COWBOY RETRIBUTION

BARB HAN

TORJAKE PUBLISHING

Editing: Ali Williams

Cover Design: Jacob's Cover Designs

To my family for unwavering love and support. I can't imagine doing life with anyone else. I love you guys with all my heart.

1

"Come on, Bear. Let's get out of here." A.J. McGannon called out to his hundred and fifty-pound Newfie. The dog was unfazed. Bear might be loyal to a fault but when he made up his mind about investigating a noise, he conveniently lost his hearing. Making kissing noises got A.J. just as ignored. But since Bear had an uncanny ability to uncover a cow or bull in trouble, A.J. had learned to trust his dog's instincts.

Nose to soil, Bear was hot and heavy on a trail. For a massive and strikingly large dog, he had the best disposition of any animal on the ranch.

The memory of finding a wounded and scared bear of a dog in the creek bed they were nearing still clenched his back teeth, even three years after the fact. The animal's back leg had been in bad shape. It was obvious based on his other wounds that he'd been in a fight or two, but he must've held his own. He'd returned to the water where he was most comfortable. A puncture wound in his left hindquarters had given him a limp. He'd been too heavy to carry, so A.J. had been forced to call for help. Ranch foreman, Hawk, brought a large wagon.

Normally, A.J. would think twice about approaching an injured animal as fierce looking as Bear. But this animal seemed to have a sixth sense and understood that A.J. was there to help.

Bear had come by his name honestly with his thick, black coat and long snout. His fur had been matted and he was all big teeth and weary eyes on the morning A.J. had found the one-year-old. The minute he'd laid eyes on the dog, A.J. had known the two of them belonged together. Life with Bear was interesting and A.J. couldn't have asked for a better animal to show up like he had three years ago.

This morning, the air was warm. Early October in Texas could bring anything from pavement scorching temperatures to long johns wearing weather.

There were the usual sounds, a breeze blowing in the trees and Ginger's, his bay mare, hooves pounding the unforgiving earth. Bear had gone ahead, and he was onto something. The dog had a sixth sense about trouble, and he was presently making a beeline for the creek, A.J. feared there might be something going wrong.

He'd pulled countless cows and bulls from a gulley

not too far from here. But that wasn't the direction Bear was headed in at the moment.

A.J. had learned a long time ago to let Bear take the lead when he was onto something. There wasn't much in life worse than an animal suffering in its last few hours on earth. A.J. took his role as cattle rancher seriously. The land wasn't just part of his heritage, it was a piece of his soul and the animals along with it.

There was no reason to suffer needlessly and getting stuck in a water ditch and slowly drowning ranked right up there. He'd seen the aftereffects and him, his brothers and his father always took it seriously.

A.J. listened for any sounds of a struggling animal. The trees were dense on this part of the ranch and since finding Bear here in the creek ahead almost three years ago, he'd made this section of the ranch part of his morning routine.

Checking fences and doing paperwork were the bane of a cattle rancher's existence but both were important. Since there were no calves to help birth or tag in the fall, making sure all the areas of the fence were secure in case the herd managed to make its way onto the outer boundaries of the property were a huge priority.

A.J. leaned forward and made a ck-ck noise before saying, "He-ya!"

Bear was bolting toward something in the creek. A.J. listened for the tell-tale sounds of a dying animal to brace himself for what he might encounter but there was nothing unusual.

"Whoa," A.J. calmed Ginger down to a walk.

Water splashed ahead and Bear was shoulder deep and charging forward. He would need a bath later; A.J. could only imagine the mud and dirt that was about to be caked in his fur. Letting him sleep at the foot of his bed had probably been a mistake but one he would repeat. Bear hadn't let A.J. out of his sight since the two had met, and to this day he refused to ride inside a vehicle.

The reason for that sent fire shooting through A.J.'s veins. The trauma of being abandoned in the country had left its marks.

"What did you find, boy?" A.J. slowed Ginger to a stop and slid off the side. He tucked the reins behind the saddle's horn. Ginger didn't spook easily, and he could trust her to stay put.

A.J. followed Bear to where he had stopped. It looked like a small tree had been knocked over, and maybe broken in the last storm. A trunk that had been carried down the creek.

"It's okay," he soothed.

Bear was sniffing something on that muddy trunk. From this distance it was hard to see what had captured his dog's interest.

As he walked closer, his pulse ramped up. The tree moved and his first thought was that it could possibly be a massive snake. That possibility was quickly quelled when a hand reached toward Bear.

Now, it was A.J.'s turn to bolt through the water and splash pretty much everything around him.

He had no idea what or who had been dumped out on his property. Normally, farmers complained of finding bodies that had been driven out and dumped from crime in bigger cities like Houston, Austin, or San Antonio. The victims were hidden in the crops and sometimes not found until harvest.

Cattle ranchers had problems with people using more remote parts of their land for trafficking. Then, there were poachers to deal with.

"My name is A.J. McGannon and you're on my family's land. I'm here to help you." He figured it couldn't hurt to identify himself to the person who was face down in the muddy bank.

As he neared, the person on the ground turned her head to the side and for the first time, he got a good look at a face.

"Tess?"

"Help me."

Those words nearly gutted A.J. and he dropped beside his neighbor. It wasn't so much the words as it was the helplessness in her tone. Tess Clemente was as fiery as she was beautiful. She was also trouble and had caused her fair share of disputes on everything from land boundaries to water supply. She had pretty

much made a career out of annoying him and his
family.

Her father owned Clemente Cattle and she ran the
family business alongside him. She had been two years
behind him in school, despite being three years
younger than him. Tess was tall, five-feet-seven-inches
if he had to guess. She was all legs and could most
likely be found wearing a minidress and boots.

Today, she had on jeans and a spaghetti strap shirt.
She looked like she'd been rolled in mud.

"I'm here." Sworn enemy or not, he wouldn't turn
his back on anyone who needed help.

"Is he gone?" Tess barely had enough energy to
speak but she needed to know if the person who'd
attacked her from behind and slipped a bag over her
head was still out there. A ripple of fear shot through
her.

Exhausted and thirsty beyond belief, she'd
managed to make her way to the creek bed where she
rolled around in the mud to blend in with the environment. She hadn't exactly been sure where she'd ended
up after breaking free from her kidnapper and running
away. She hadn't looked back and that meant she didn't
have a good description of the man who'd attacked
her.

Seeing A.J., the one McGannon who usually got so

far on her nerves she would rather stomp out of a room than look at him, was an oddly welcomed relief.

She might not generally like to be in his presence, but he was a good person. He wouldn't let anyone hurt her. He would get her to safety.

A.J. surveyed the area as his hand went to the pistol that was holstered in his belt. It was common practice for ranchers to carry weapons in these parts. Wild hogs roamed and there were other dangers, both animal and human.

Again, poachers were a real problem for ranchers and had become even more ruthless since poaching penalties had become stiffer. A person with everything to lose wasn't a good person to run into out on land that stretched out for hundreds of acres.

And yet, Tess wished it had been a poacher who'd attacked her. Something hinted that would have been far less dangerous.

"I don't see anyone." A.J. returned his pistol to his holster. "Let's get you out of here."

She nodded, and then he helped her up. Her limbs felt like concrete weights. Thankfully, A.J. was strong. He had that whole muscled and toned bit down to a T. There weren't many men she could think of off-hand that were more attractive than A.J.; if only his personality matched that outside. Or he would actually listen to reason instead of being bull-headed when she came to him with a complaint about trees on his property that were wreaking havoc on her equipment building because they'd been planted too close. Then, there was the water shortage and the fact that he couldn't keep his cattle out of her meadow.

Right now, though, she couldn't be happier to see a McGannon. Bear had scared the bejesus out of her when she first opened her eyes to see the huge black dog.

Her knees were like rubber bands, so standing on her own was going to be impossible. When she nearly went down again, his strong hands held her upright.

"I don't want to hurt you. Mind if I pick you up?" he asked.

Her body was too weak to make it all the way to his horse. She'd lost track of how long she'd been out here alone. Torrential rain had made it impossible to know when it was day or night and she'd lost her phone when she'd been attacked.

"What day is it?" she managed to ask but darkness was tugging at her. She'd used up all her remaining energy talking and trying to walk.

"Thursday. What happened?"

"Sheriff. My father." Those were the last words she remembered saying before everything went dark again.

TESS BLINKED OPEN BLURRY EYES. A headache raged. The kind that hurt the backs of her eyes.

"Drink this." A.J. McGannon sat at her bedside, holding a glass of water in his hands.

She managed to sit up.

"Thank you." Her mouth was as dry and cracked as East Texas soil. A few sips helped ease some of the dryness. Talking made her lips hurt. "Do you have any ChapStick?"

"My sister-in-law put together a few things she thought you could use." He picked up a small basket from the nightstand and then set it on the bed.

She looked through the lotion, breath mints and found something for dry lips. She applied it and picked up a granola bar.

Didn't A.J. tell her that it was Thursday?

"My father will be worried sick. Has anyone tried to reach him?"

A.J.'s face twisted up like he was offended. "We might have our differences, but we wouldn't hold something like this from your family."

"I didn't mean—"

He waved her off as he picked up his phone and fired off a text.

"The sheriff asked me to let her know when you were awake. She's been trying to reach your father, but he hasn't returned her calls," A.J. supplied.

"Oh, right. I almost forgot that he's in Dallas. My dad and cell phones never were a good match, so he might not remember to check." Technology and her dad weren't friends. They weren't even acquaintances.

He only carried a cell because she practically forced him to. As he was getting older, she didn't want him out on the ranch by himself, as he often was, with no way to contact home if something happened. "He's a good man but he can be so stubborn."

"What happened to you? How'd you get lost and end up on our property?" Based on the sharp words they'd had in the past, A.J. would know she hadn't crossed the boundary on purpose.

"I didn't realize I'd been taken here in the first place." She needed to get a grip on her defensiveness. It was foreign having a conversation with A.J. that didn't start as an argument. The concern lines etched in his forehead reminded her that he wasn't there to make her life harder.

In fact, he'd probably just saved her life.

"Thank you," she said quickly. "If you hadn't shown when you did, I'm not sure what might have happened."

"You can thank Bear for that. I might've ridden right on past."

She must've made a face without realizing because he put a hand up.

"Hold on. I didn't mean that I wasn't glad to find you. I'd just like to know how you ended up there and in the condition you're in."

"Someone jumped me from behind. I have no idea who. Locking the door to the barn is the last thing I remember before waking up with some kind of bag over my head. Everything was dark and," her voice broke, "sorry. I don't mean to get emotional."

"Don't be. You've been through one hell of an experience. A less strong person wouldn't be here right now." His words had a calming effect despite the fact the two of them usually threw verbal jabs at each other. This was a nice change.

"Thank you, A.J." She hesitated. "That's really nice coming from someone like you."

Okay, she didn't mean to light a fire in him but that's exactly what happened. A storm brewed behind those hazel and brown eyes of his. To most, he would be intimidating with his six-feet-four-inch frame and muscles that had muscles. His hair was so dark brown that it was almost black.

So, yeah, he could seem threatening.

Tess also knew the man had principles and honor, something that seemed missing in too many of the men she'd dated in the past couple of years. Most of her dates seemed more interested in what was happening on the phone's screen than in her. Phones came out at the dinner table, at the lake, and in the car. One guy leaned in for a goodnight kiss while they were still in his vehicle and a text caught his attention first. He'd stopped mid-lean.

So, as much as she would never be attracted to A.J. McGannon, she had to admit that it was nice to be around someone who knew how to put his phone down and pay attention in a conversation.

He hadn't once checked his cell except to let the sheriff know she was awake. And then he'd set it down without looking twice.

It was probably because he'd shown up in her time of crisis that she was seeing so many things to appreciate about A.J. and not the niggle of attraction she felt toward him the minute he'd looked into her eyes.

At least, that was the lie she tried to sell herself while her heart pounded in her chest.

2

M iss Penny knocked on the open door to the guest suite.

"Come in." A.J. glanced at Tess before turning to the family's lifeline. Miss Penny had taken care of A.J., his brothers and cousins after his mother had died. They'd been a handful, but she'd kept everyone in line.

The woman who'd become a second mother had to be in her mid- to late-sixties despite having the energy of a twenty-five-year-old. The best description he'd heard of her was that she was tiny but mighty.

Miss Penny also came with a warning label. She might be petite and have a natural skip to her step when she walked, but everyone knew better than to cross her. Of course, she was the kind of person who'd earned their respect long ago.

Her salt and pepper hair had been in the exact

same style for A.J.'s entire life, short and feathered to one side. But it was Miss Penny's clear green eyes that could see right through a person. For most of his life, he'd seen her in a blouse with jeans, often wearing her favorite apron that spelled out the word, *BOSS*.

"The sheriff is here. She said you called." Miss Penny's gaze held on Tess and there were questions dancing in those green eyes of hers.

"Thank you. I'll explain later, or you're welcome to sit in while Tess gives her statement," he said to Miss Penny.

"No explanation needed. I'm headed to the hospital with Hawk." Hawk was the ranch foreman. His nickname came from the fact nothing got past him. He was fairly close in age with Miss Penny, a few years younger, and it hadn't gotten past any of A.J.'s brothers the two had been spending a lot of time together since their dad's hospitalization. "Any friend of yours is always welcome here."

Miss Penny had placed careful emphasis on the word, *friend.*

"I appreciate it, but—"

Before he could explain that Tess wasn't his friend, Miss Penny lifted a hand up to stop him. It was probably for the best anyway. He'd already stuck his boot in his mouth and offended her once.

"It's nice to see neighbors who step in to help each other and actually get along," Miss Penny said almost under her breath.

"Is there any way we can talk to the sheriff in the kitchen?" Tess seemed to decide to leave the comment alone, but her chin tilted, and she looked at Miss Penny with understanding and something else...appreciation?

A.J. decided not to put too much stock in it. Once this was over, Tess Clemente would go right back to being her usual thorn in the side self.

"I'll see her in and set her up with a cup of coffee," Miss Penny answered before A.J. could. He chuckled to himself. It was easy to see who was really in charge. Apparently, there was no 'off' button when it came to parenting, no matter how old he got. At thirty-two-years-old, he'd believe himself to be immune.

"Thank you, Miss Penny." Tess's show of respect earned points with the woman.

Miss Penny smiled. "There are clean clothes in the bathroom. Should be a jogging suit about your size. We've collected plenty over the years and no one would mind if you wanted to borrow one."

Tess thanked Miss Penny for a second time.

"I'll see the sheriff in and be on my way." The older woman turned around and then disappeared down the hallway.

"I'm surprised she didn't hold the cup of water under your mouth so you could drink," A.J. teased.

"Are you jealous?" Tess's full pink lips formed a thin line.

There was no way he was giving her the satisfaction. Although, the break in tension was a welcomed relief.

"Exactly how much help do you need in the bathroom? I can be pretty handy removing clothes," he quipped and then realized what that must sound like. "I didn't mean—"

"Oh, sure you didn't." Her cheeks flamed despite the fact she was trying to act all cool about his slip. He had to admit she looked beautiful with the coloring.

"I'm trying to be serious here." He needed to shut down that line of thinking. Kidding or not, his heart drummed his rib cage the way this conversation was going. This was not the time nor the place to flirt. And, more importantly, not the person to flirt with. "Do you need my help getting into the other room? I can move this chair inside, so you don't have to stand while you clean up."

She stared him down for a long moment.

Being stubborn was one thing but being stupid was another. Tess Clemente had stubbornness in spades, she most definitely was not stupid. "Actually, that would be nice," she conceded, even though it looked like it pained her to admit to needing the help.

He stood and picked up the chair he'd been sitting in. Getting through the bathroom door without raking his knuckles proved difficult but he managed.

Tess was sitting on the edge of the bed with her toes on the floor by the time he got back to her. Her face was flush as she held a hand up.

"I better move slowly."

"You said someone came up from behind. Is it possible this person gave you something? Rohypnol?" The date-rape drug would have knocked her out and made her pliant. Of course, chloroform would knock her out the fastest, making it a distinct possibility.

"I know I didn't take anything." She looked down at her arms for signs of a break in skin from a needle, rubbing her arms to clear some of the mud off. "I don't see any marks."

"Take it easy when you try to stand." He walked over and offered an arm. "We can move as slowly as you need to."

His mind was spinning. Her dad was out of town and he didn't know her ranch hands very well. He believed they ran a tight ship at Clemente Cattle. As much as he didn't like her and her father, he'd never heard a bad word spoken about either one in town.

If her father made a practice of hiring hands that were bad news, word would've gotten around. One of the things A.J. liked about living and working in Cattle Cove was the fact people knew each other.

And, yes, at times people could be a little too much in each other's business but folks generally meant well. In a small ranching community, people were known to pull together to help each other out and relied on neighbors to get the word around.

Of course, technology and advances in equipment made ranchers more self-reliant than ever. But folks here still kept in touch the old-fashioned way by going into town on Sundays and meeting up at the park or for breakfast at Odie's Place and talking.

A.J. and his brothers were exceptions. They preferred staying on the ranch and out of gossip's way.

"I'm sorry about your father," Tess said as she tried to stand. Her body tensed and she gripped his arm like a vise.

The comment caught him off guard.

"I heard what happened and I've been meaning to stop by but..."

"You don't have to do this." He cut her off as she seemed to be thinking of a reason.

"What?" She seemed genuinely confused.

"Pretend that you're worried about my dad."

"We may have had disagreements over the years, but you can't think I'd want something like this to happen to him." Her words rushed out and the heated look in her honey-brown eyes caught him off guard.

"That's not what I was saying. Look, I'm not communicating well." The fact she was reading him wrong didn't help. "I appreciate your concern for Dad."

"He's a good man," she said defensively. There'd be no argument from A.J. "And he doesn't deserve to have something like this happen to him."

"Thank you."

"Is it true your Uncle Donny was with him when it happened?" She leaned some of her weight on him and they took a couple of forward steps.

"Yes."

"You know, I never liked him." Again, there'd be no argument from him on her bold statement.

"Turns out we agree on at least one thing."

This close to her, he didn't want to overthink the heat pinging between them. Or the fact that he wanted to help her more than he cared to admit.

TESS FELT a jolt of electricity at the point of contact with A.J. with every forward step she took. The sensation caught her off guard. She didn't want to feel anything but gratitude toward him. She meant what she'd said about his father. Clive McGannon was a decent man. Not only had he brought up his six sons after their mother passed away, but he'd raised his brother's boys too.

Eleven boys under one roof. Growing up an only child, she couldn't imagine such a clan. She had a half-brother who lived in Houston. Hudson Leonard ran a successful logistics business out of Galveston, he was six months older than Tess and rarely came to the ranch. His mother had asked for full custody and her father hadn't fought her on it.

Tess had one thing in common with A.J. They'd both been brought up by their fathers. A.J.'s mother had died not long after his youngest brother was born, while hers had taken off after learning about Hudson.

She never looked back, either. Tess had no idea if the woman was alive or dead.

A part of her wanted to know what had happened to her mother. The other, more dominant part had believed any woman who could walk away from her child without so much as sending a card on her birthday didn't want or deserve to be found.

So, yeah, she had a stick up her craw about her dear mother. Her father never spoke about Nicole Clemente and there were no pictures of her in the house. Tess had been told she favored her mother in a lot of ways, but she'd never been certain if it was meant as a compliment.

Tess had grown up with a loving, doting father and he'd hired a service who supplied a new nanny every few years. Some were from Europe and weren't old enough to buy alcohol in the U.S. As soon as Tess had been old enough to drive, she'd ordered a meal service for her and her father and asked him to ditch the nannies as soon as the last one's contract expired. She'd expected a fight, but he'd obliged. There really hadn't been a need for live-in care once Tess was old enough to take care of herself.

Thankfully, he'd seen the light. Then again, there wasn't much he'd denied his only daughter. Tess had never needed much and certainly didn't ask for expensive things. Being brought up in a wealthy ranching family kept her grounded. Ranchers were the most down-to-earth people.

"I meant what I said about your dad." She eased onto the chair in the bathroom that was next to the sink. "We may have had our differences but he's a really good human being."

"Thanks for that."

"What does your uncle say happened?" She winced as she tried to lean toward the sink. A quick glance in the mirror shocked her back to reality. Mud was caked in her hair and pretty much covering most of her face. It was already in her clothes and stuck pretty much everywhere else it could find an opening. She used a wet washcloth that A.J. provided to wipe it out of her ear.

"Says he didn't see anything."

She made a guffaw noise. "Are you kidding me right now?"

Based on the scowl on A.J.'s face any time he spoke about his uncle, she could tell he didn't believe the line any more than she did. She could only imagine what that must be doing to the tightknit crew. Five of the boys Clive McGannon had raised were his brother's sons.

"That's the story he's sticking to," A.J. said, making it clear that he didn't buy it. He wet another washcloth and brought it over to her along with a fresh towel.

"What does the sheriff think?" Not that any of this was her business. She was in the McGannon home and her curiosity about them was piqued. Being here gave her a foreign sense of comfort. She didn't expect to like it here as much as she did or feel such a pull toward someone she'd spent the past few years arguing with.

The attraction she felt toward A.J. was probably just some weird syndrome because he'd literally saved her life. There couldn't be anything more to it than basic biology. And she was certain once the shock of being attacked and then nearly dehydrating wore off so would the inconvenient pull toward a man who might be gorgeous and intelligent but was certainly not her type.

"She brought Uncle Donny in for another interview. She seems to have questions."

"And what about your family? What do your brothers think? And how are your cousins dealing with all this?" She realized she'd just rapid-fired questions at him a little too late to reel them back in. What happened with his siblings was none of her business. Except that A.J.'s father had always been fair in their dealings and she'd never heard a bad word spoken about him in town. "Sorry. You don't have to answer any of those questions."

A.J. chuckled, mostly to himself, and he didn't respond.

"What?" She balked.

"You sure have a lot of interest in my family," he said.

"Not really. I'm just here and figured I might as well ask." Honestly, it was a lot easier to focus on something else, *anything* else than it was to think about her situation. Her head still hurt and her mind still reeled. Any distraction was a welcomed change.

"I texted Dr. Setter while you were resting. She should be here any minute." The change of subject didn't go unnoticed. It was fair that he probably didn't want to discuss something so personal with her anyway. The two of them had never been friends or friendly for that matter. He was helping her purely out of honor.

"Thanks. That was considerate. I might have been hit in the head." She reached her hand to the crown of her head and felt around. Her fingers landed on a goose egg-sized knot that hurt the minute she touched it. "Ouch."

"Between my brothers and cousins, I have a lot of experience with concussions." A.J. sat down on the edge of the massive tub. "Do you know your name?"

"Tess Clemente. And are you kidding me? We just had a conversation about your family. I know who I am. The day of the week confused me because it's been raining outside, and it was impossible to tell light from day. This happened on Tuesday and you said it's Thursday, which basically means I've been out of it for almost two days. I was thirsty and hungry when you found me, which was nothing in comparison to the headache I had and was probably the reason I felt sick to my stomach. You and I have never been friends but that didn't stop you from helping me, which, by the way, you reminded me that your dog is probably the reason I'm alive right now. Does that about cover it?"

He sat there for a long moment, studying her and she suddenly felt self-conscious.

"It does for me," he said before getting up and walking out of the room.

3

"I'm sorry for what I said in the bathroom."

The doctor was right behind Tess as she walked into the kitchen. She'd washed off the mud, pulled her hair off her face, and had on a fresh jogging suit. It was no doubt the one Miss Penny had mentioned.

"I'll get back to you with the results," Setter quietly said to the sheriff before handing over a sealed bag with Tess's clothes inside.

It dawned on A.J. that the doctor would be talking about sexual assault. His hands fisted.

"Not a problem," he said to Tess. The doctor had arrived a few minutes after he walked out and joined the sheriff. He'd shown her to the bathroom where she said she could examine Tess in private. A.J. figured the sooner he helped her with her statement to the sheriff and had the doctor give her the green light to go home, the better.

But now he felt like a jerk for wanting to rush her out the door. He looked to the sheriff, who was seated at the large hand-carved dining table in the kitchen nursing a cup of coffee as she finished talking to the doctor.

Setter turned to Tess. "If you need anything, you know how to reach me."

"Yes. Thank you," Tess responded.

A.J. showed the doctor out and then returned to the kitchen.

"Sheriff," he said as he moved to get his own cup. Hours had passed since he'd found Tess and he was ready to get to the bottom of the situation. The fact she'd been attacked on her own land while her father was out of town didn't sit well. Since he didn't know her ranch hands, his thoughts shifted there first.

But why take her away from the main house and not kill her? The implication nailed him in the gut because it meant whoever had taken her had meant to keep her alive for a little while before killing her.

Taking her out onto the edge of her property and onto his brought his family into the situation. McGannons took crimes on their land very seriously. His newly minted sister-in-law, Alexis, who'd just married his brother, Ryan, had been renting out the cabin that A.J. was managing when a killer struck. Technically, they'd had a wedding promise ceremony. The civil ceremony would wait until their father woke from the coma that he'd been in for weeks now.

Her boss had orchestrated the murders to cover the fact that he'd been milking his and his wife's company out of money—money he'd planned to use to build his new life after he divorced her.

Alexis and Ryan had reconnected and were now married, but she was still dealing with the loss of her friends, as she would be for a long time. Death wasn't something a person got over in a few weeks.

"Can you tell me what happened, Miss Clemente?" Sheriff Laney Justice asked.

Tess recounted the story just like she'd told A.J.

"What about your cell phone?" Sheriff Justice asked. A.J. realized why. She wanted to trace the phone's location in hopes it would lead her to the perp.

"I had it on me, but it's gone now." She folded her arms. "Maybe it's near the area where I was attacked."

"Are there any security cameras in place on your property? Particularly around your barn?" Sheriff Justice asked.

"There's never been a need for them before now," Tess said defensively. He understood why she'd react that way. This town was small and people looked out for each other. Until recently, most folks left their keys in their vehicles while parked outside a restaurant or shopping in town. Almost no one ever locked their houses. This meant their entire way of life was in jeopardy. They'd grown up in a place where crime rarely existed.

One could make the argument that that ship had sailed lately, but it was always different when it hit this close to home.

Poachers were an issue on the land. They never came close to the house. Violence had always been an *out there* problem. Poachers were dangerous not stupid. Risking getting caught by coming too close to town would be an amateur move, which they weren't.

Besides, they were after livestock, not people.

This person seemed to have his sights on Tess, which made A.J. wonder just how well she knew the people who worked on her dad's ranch.

"I understand." The sheriff had been through several criminal investigations in recent months in addition to still trying to figure out what happened to A.J.'s father and if criminal charges might end up needing to be filed. That was the word circulating around after the third interview with Uncle Donny. "Have you hired anyone new at your place of business?"

"No. We've had the same hands for years. The newest is nicknamed Doolittle for how good he is with all animals. We hired him five years ago." Why did it bother A.J. that she had a nickname for one of the ranch hands? What happened on the Clemente ranch was none of his business.

"I'd still like to talk to your employees. See if

anyone heard anything on the night of the abduction." The last word was barely out of the sheriff's mouth when Tess's muscles tensed.

"How do you take your coffee?" he asked, wanting to provide what little comfort he could. A normal routine or a simple beverage could make a difference during intense situations, he'd noticed. All he ever did was drink coffee and pace the halls at the hospital when it was his turn to take a shift watching out for their dad. If Clive McGannon woke from his coma, he would have someone who loved him at the ready. The family was big enough to have him covered around the clock.

"A little cream if you have it and one sugar." The grateful look she shot him pierced his armor. His chest took a hit.

He didn't respond for fear his voice would give away the effect she'd just had on him. Being around her already stirred up a mess of damn confusing feelings—and A.J. didn't normally *do* feelings.

Seeing her helpless the way he'd found her and then again as the doctor spoke to the sheriff about a possible sexual assault was bound to break down some of his walls. Especially when he was used to seeing her all fire and determination when she argued about property lines if a new piece of fence had to be put up, or who owned water rights to a particular well. Her personality suited her, and he had a sense that he would actually like to hang around with her if they weren't so contentious in most of their conversations. He still wasn't certain just how he'd drawn the short straw on being the one designated to talk to her. He also appreciated the fact most of their interactions happened over the phone. Being in the same room with her was distracting.

Thankfully, issues didn't come up a whole lot, and the ones that did were normally resolved as quickly as humanly possible. He'd never seen any sense in dragging out a dispute.

But it wasn't their history that had him interested in her now. As he walked over to hand her a cup of coffee, there was a small patch of mud that she'd missed near her left temple close to her hairline that he'd like to help her with.

Since that would probably be about as productive as trying to bottle feed a beetle, he shelved the instinct to reach out and touch her.

"One sugar with a little cream." He handed over the mug and took a seat across the table from her.

The sheriff was seated at the end of the table and she had out a notebook. "We'll want to canvas the area near where Miss Clemente was found. See if there are any clues as to who might have done this."

"Please, call me Tess," she interrupted, bringing her fingers up to her temples and massaging them like she was staving off a headache.

The sheriff nodded and repeated the name.

"You already know we'll cooperate fully with any

investigation, Sheriff." It couldn't hurt to have law enforcement around. Uncle Donny seemed nervous any time Sheriff Justice was in the room. "You can have full access to the property, barns, buildings. Anything you need."

Sheriff Justice thanked him.

"I can take you to the area where I found her." He remembered it distinctly because of the creek. He turned to Tess when he asked, "Do you have any idea how far you moved from your original position in the woods?"

She shook her head. "I know my ranch but never venture off our property except to head into town for supplies or go to Austin. Even those trips have been cut way back considering most anything I need can be delivered these days."

A.J. brought out a map of the property. It was rough and needed updating but would do for now. He set it on the table so everyone could easily view it.

"I found her here." He touched the spot in the creek and looked up in time to see Tess shiver.

"I was so close to the property line of my ranch." She could hear the disbelief in her own voice. She had to work to make herself sit at the table and look at the spot. Seeing the area made it feel like a dozen fire ants crawled across her skin.

Fire raged through her at the thought she'd been attacked so close to home. The sheriff had used the word *abducted* and it had struck a nerve in Tess. She'd considered being attacked but the word abducted had a more sinister connotation, and one she hadn't quite considered before.

She tried to shake off the heavy thoughts and refocus.

Thankfully, she'd been able to escape. She could only imagine the horrors the man had planned for her. At least, she assumed her abductor had been a man. Whoever it was had been strong enough to carry her.

"How certain are you the person worked alone?" the sheriff asked.

"When I came to, I only heard one set of footsteps outside of the camp. I woke to find myself in a small manmade hut. I would have been able to reach out and touch the walls on each side if my wrists weren't bound behind my back." She paused long enough to issue a sharp breath before continuing. "I managed to look through the branches and, when I didn't see anyone, I got out of there."

"The bindings on your wrists, do you recall what they were made of?" the sheriff asked.

"Yeah, baling twine just like we use around the barn."

"What does that mean to you?" A.J. asked the sheriff.

"The crime was premeditated and could have

involved someone who had access to the barn," she stated.

"My thoughts exactly," he agreed.

"Hold on a minute. No one at Clemente Cattle would do this to me, I'm certain of that," she defended. There was no doubt in her mind that she could trust their employees. "Besides, why now?"

"I was going to say the same thing," A.J. said. "My first thought was her employees." He held a hand up in defense. "But that's because I don't know them."

"Every ranch hand who can't account for his whereabouts on Tuesday night is a suspect, including yours." The sheriff issued a pointed look toward A.J.

He put his hands up in the surrender position.

"Hawk will know where each of his employees were on the night in question." A.J. seemed to have no doubts about that.

"I'm not done there. Any male who has access to baling twine is on my list." That statement seemed to fire up A.J.

"That means you just accused me, my brothers and cousins," he said sharply.

"Not exactly," she defended.

"You might as well have." He tapped his index finger on the table. "And every other male in the country who is strong enough to lift Tess."

"If it makes you feel any better, I'm including shop owners—"

"No, it really doesn't. Because that suspect list is

huge and it will take you and your deputies weeks, and possibly even months, to interview all those people." The thought of a lengthy investigation while this jerk roamed free sent an icy shiver down Tess's back.

"Do you have a better idea?" She locked onto his gaze, issuing a challenge.

"Yes. Arrest the bastard who did this before it happens to someone else's neighbor, daughter or sister." A.J. pushed to standing and started pacing. He raked his fingers through thick, dark hair. He had just enough stubble on his face to be considered sexy, and he had sex appeal in spades. It didn't help that he was rather passionately defending her at the moment.

Tess didn't want to like A.J., not in that sense. He'd earned her gratitude and even her respect, but she didn't want to be interested in him as more than acquaintances. She especially couldn't afford to have her heart stirring in the way that it had when he'd defended her.

"We could move the process along a lot faster if everyone cooperates," the sheriff said.

"You already know we will do everything we can to help. Tell me what you need." A.J. slowed his pace as he made another lap around the granite island.

Tess had never been inside the big house until now. Everything about it was, well, big. But the place was far more beautiful than she'd imagined. The massive wooden table where she currently sat looked reclaimed and like it had been hand carved; it also sat no less than a dozen people and she was reminded of just how big his family was. Between his brothers and cousins, it wouldn't be hard to fill every seat. Tess couldn't imagine how much food this group would've taken down as hungry teenagers.

"I'd like to set up an interview room here," she said.

"Done." There was no hesitation on A.J.'s part. "We can line up my guys first. I guess that's only fair considering she was found on our land."

Tess didn't for once think either ranch would hire shady characters, and she refused to panic and falsely accuse anyone. Despite their differences of opinion, she had always respected the McGannons, as had her father. Speaking of whom, she guessed the sheriff hadn't had any luck reaching him or he would've tried to contact her.

Which reminded her that she needed to leave him a voicemail. Not that he would listen, but he would see that she'd called and call her back.

"I'll round up the men. Do you want to work in here or in the office?" he asked.

"I'd prefer to be somewhere I can have some privacy," she said. "I'd like to call in Deputy Tucker if there's a place he can work. We'll cut the interview time in half that way."

"I can set him up in the barn office if that's agreeable." A.J.'s offer was met with a nod.

"While that's all being set up, I'd like to visit the

site." Sheriff Justice pointed to the spot in the creek where A.J. had found Tess.

Another shiver raced up her arms. Ignoring it and every other warning bell sounding in her head, she said, "I'd like to go see it for myself."

The sheriff's lips compressed.

"I'm coming," A.J. said and it was more like a warning. The warning being that the sheriff should think twice before refusing his request. "It will take a little while to round up my men anyway. I'll let Hawk know the game plan. I'm guessing you'll want to interview him as well. Knowing Hawk, he'll want to go first to show his men there's nothing to worry about."

Instead of arguing, she conceded. "I guess that would be all right. As long as everything is in place when we get back from the site. What's the fastest route to get to the creek?"

"This path right here." He walked over to the map and pointed. "And the fastest way to get there is to use ATVs."

The sheriff looked at him with the most serious eyes. "I'm ready when you are."

4

"Do you want your own ATV, or do you feel safe riding with me?"

The question wasn't whether or not Tess felt safe riding with A.J. It was, *did she want to be that close to him?* The electrical impulses firing between them were embarrassing and she didn't want to give away her body's reaction to someone she'd viewed as an adversary for most of her adult life.

"I'll be okay. I'd rather be on back than take the wheel right now." Her head had been threatening a headache, and he knew the area better than she did. "Take it easy, though."

He shot her a look. "I'm not here to make you hurt worse than you already do."

She ducked her head, chin to chest, to cover her embarrassment at the off-handed comment. "Sorry for how that sounded. I didn't mean it like that."

Thankfully, he let it go as he retrieved a pair of helmets and handed one to her and the other to the sheriff. His was strapped onto the back of his ATV, which he climbed onto first before offering Tess a hand. Considering their history, A.J. was probably holding his tongue a lot. He must want to fire off a snappy comeback like he usually did when she pushed his buttons.

After securing the helmet, she took his hand and followed his lead onto the vehicle. Not leaning into him and wrapping her arms around him to secure herself would draw more attention to her, so she bit the bullet.

Clasping her hands around his broad, muscled chest, she ignored the electricity vibrating through her arms. The sound of the engine covered the deep breath she'd taken in. A shower sounded nice about then. She could only imagine what she must smell like despite freshening up earlier and brushing her teeth.

But that wasn't her biggest concern at the moment. Facing the creek again sent her mind into a spiral. Anxiety tightened her chest, making it feel like her shirt was about four sizes too small. Reminding herself to breathe through it, she closed her eyes.

It felt like it took an hour, but the creek was probably forty-minutes away by ATV. A.J. had contacted Hawk to update him on the situation before leaving the house and the foreman was rounding up the hands. If all went well, Sheriff Justice planned to have all the interviews finished this evening.

The ATV finally came to a stop after bouncing around. She realized A.J. had done his best to take a smooth route.

Being back out on ranch property and so close to home shouldn't cause her chest to squeeze, but it felt like every breath was a real effort and her lungs were seizing. Tess reminded herself to take this one step at a time.

All she needed to do was to walk over to the creek. She'd handle it by putting one foot in front of the other. Taking that first step was always the hardest and her feet seemed rooted to the ground.

"This way." A.J. seemed to pick up on her tension. He reached for her hand and took it in his. There was something about the connection, the skin-to-skin contact, that calmed her frazzled nerves and gave her the courage to take a couple of steps closer to the creek bed.

The sheriff was quiet as she seemed to take in every part of the area surrounding the creek.

"Can you show me exactly where and how you found her?" she asked A.J.

He nodded and closed the distance between them and the creek. "She was here, face down, looking more like a log or tree branch than a human being."

The sheriff knelt down beside the spot.

"Which direction did you come from?" she asked.

"East." A.J. pointed toward a grouping of trees. "I hopped off Ginger right about there and that's where she stayed."

"You said Bear located Tess."

"That's right."

"And he would've come from the same direction. East?" The sheriff had locked onto something on the north side of the creek.

"He'd been with me all morning, so, yes," A.J. confirmed.

"And you found Tess around six o'clock in the morning."

"Yes." He moved closer and Tess caught sight of what the sheriff had locked onto. A single set of footprints walking toward the creek bed.

Her heart galloped, pounding her rib cage as the three of them followed the trail. She'd been *abducted*, to use the sheriff's word, Tuesday evening and found Thursday at six a.m. So, how long had she been out of it?

It had rained and then stopped. It had felt like days but might have been mere hours. She'd taken a serious blow to the head, the evidence of which was a pumpknot that had formed on the crown of her skull.

Being here caused an eerie feeling to creep over her, like a cat walking over her grave. She tightened her grip on A.J.'s hand and he brushed his thumb over hers causing all kinds of sensations to rock her body.

Backtracking, using her footsteps on a trail she

barely remembered taking, sent a cold chill down her spine. She was grateful for the rain now, though. It hadn't rained hard enough to wash away the evidence of her route.

Instead, it was the reason they had footsteps to track. A few deep breaths later, and her heart calmed down a few notches below panic. Shock of all shocks, it was A.J. McGannon's presence that was helping her the most. If someone had told her that he'd be a calming force in her life at some point she would've laughed in their face.

Following the trail she'd left for them, the sheriff, who was fifteen feet in front of them, abruptly stopped. Tess was pretty certain she heard the woman mutter a curse.

"Stay back," the sheriff said as she took out her phone and started snapping pics.

Curiosity got the best of Tess and there was no way she was standing back when the area might jog her memory. It was probably the blow she'd taken to the head that had caused temporary memory loss. She'd read an article about it the last time she'd gone in for a physical and had been left waiting in the exam room.

Temporary memory loss of events that happened right before trauma was not uncommon according to the article. She'd thought the information was interesting and filed it away almost as quickly as she'd learned it.

In her daily life, concussions were rare and temporary memory loss from head trauma was even rarer. The only reason she'd picked up the article in the first place was thinking that one of the ranch hands might get bucked off a horse or end up with an injury like A.J.'s father had received.

It was a shame that Clive McGannon was in a hospital bed unable to say what happened to him. Donny McGannon didn't have the best reputation but was he a murderer?

She thought she remembered him being the one who'd called for an ambulance. Would he do that if he'd been the one to strike?

He could've had a bout of guilt after the fact. She hoped the sheriff was looking into the man's finances to be certain.

Thinking about Mr. McGannon kept her mind off the horror she walked up to. She grabbed A.J.'s arm with her free hand. Instinct kicked in and she moved behind him, using him to shield her from what she saw.

A makeshift campsite was there. And so was a noose.

SHOCK DIDN'T BEGIN to cover A.J.'s reaction to the camp that had been made on his family's land. He'd come across a lot of disturbing sites out on the ranch over the years, but this took the cake.

The best word he could think of to describe it was deranged.

There was a ready-made hut in the center of a small clearing. The trees were fairly thick on this part of the property except for this area. Leaves had been gathered up and piled into a circle around the hut that was made of tree branches and stones.

It looked like the place had been abandoned in a hurry and that the person who made it was too fearful to come back and destroy his creation. Of course, he might be bold enough to think no one would find it. And the other option was that he was somewhere out there watching even now.

Maybe the guy got his rocks off that way.

A.J. tightened his grip on Tess's hand. He wanted to protect her from view of the site but also realized she was a victim and the only witness. Maybe being there could spark a memory that could put the bastard behind bars.

Speaking of bars, he fished his cell out of his pocket and checked for service. Had none.

The sheriff's radio range seemed better. Her face was tilted to one side and she was talking into a mouthpiece in between photo sessions.

A.J. scanned the trees, looking for any signs of the bastard responsible for this. He knew enough about a crime scene not to get any closer. The sheriff had what looked like a garment tape out in the next few seconds, measuring footprints and then recording her findings.

A half hour passed before she came over to talk.

"There's a lot to process here," she said.

"What can you tell so far from the scene?" She might not tell him anything, but it never hurt to ask.

"That one person is responsible for the crime. There's only one set of footprints aside from Tess's. He'd planned to kill her based on the noose but not before he punished her in some way." She shot an apologetic glance at Tess. "I'm sorry. This must sound scary and cold to you. Profiling the man responsible for this will help us know where to concentrate our efforts."

"Does this guy have a grudge against Tess?" he asked.

"That or a fixation. The hut could symbolize their 'home' that he envisioned. He obviously likes the woods and the leaves must mean something. Right now, the picture is still blurry, but this gives us a lot to work with," the sheriff said.

This furthered his thinking that Tess shouldn't go home to her ranch until this jerk was caught. She would argue the point, but he had every intention of lobbying a case for his opinion. Then again, based on the way she'd tucked herself behind him, this scene did its damage.

He'd talk to her about finding new accommodations, at least until her father returned from Dallas and the meetings he had there.

She'd been vague about what her father was doing

out of town. Of course, she had no reason to confide in A.J. even though a little piece of him liked the breakthrough they seemed to be having more than he probably should. This was more like a shattering of the barriers that had them constantly on the other side of issues.

He told himself that dealing with her on ranch business would be a helluva lot easier if they had a tentative relationship and a baseline of trust. He also told himself that he would help anyone in a crisis— and that much was true.

What he couldn't easily write off was how right it felt to hold her hand or stand so close he could almost feel her breathing.

His thoughts were interrupted by the sheriff's next question.

"Do you know anyone who has a grudge against you?" she asked Tess.

Tess stood there for a moment. Every muscle in her body had gone rigid and he felt it through her hand. He also felt her heart beating wildly, so he tugged her closer to him and looped his arms around her. She sidestepped, which put her in front of him. Then, she grabbed hold of his clasped hands before leaning into him, her back to his chest.

Now, he could really feel her heartbeat. He could also feel her body as it trembled. Despite facing what must be the most horrific memory, her chin was held high.

Pride surged.

"I can't think of anyone off-hand who would want to torture me but that obviously doesn't mean that he doesn't exist."

"There's another possibility. That he somehow wanted to play house with you. The hut might represent a fantasy that the two of you would be a couple. Have you noticed anyone stopping by the house without a reason or showing up in town at the same places as you?"

She shrugged. "No one that I can think of."

"Let me know if you think of anyone," the sheriff said. "What about dates? Has anyone asked you out recently?"

Tess was beautiful and intelligent, and when she wasn't coming at him with fire and flames, she was incredibly attractive. He could only imagine the number of men ready to line up for a chance at a date with her.

"Not lately, no. I've been on a break after the last guy I dated, who turned out to be a jerk. Honestly, I've been taking a little time off from the whole dating scene," she admitted.

His loss. A.J. bit back the comment on his tongue.

"And I haven't noticed anyone hanging around unusually, but I do come into contact with the opposite sex a lot during my days at the ranch. I go into town to run errands frequently because my dad's getting older and I take on as much work around the ranch as I can to relieve him. Oh, and I drive to Austin every other week to volunteer at a crisis center there," she stated.

The more he got to know Tess, the more he realized he'd underestimated her before. He'd viewed her as someone who'd grown up with a silver spoon in her mouth, a princess who always had to get her way.

He never would have believed she drove all the way to Austin every other week to volunteer or that she worked so hard to take the load off her father's back. A.J. respected her even more now.

"What's the name of the crisis center where you volunteer in Austin?" the sheriff asked.

"AustinCares. It's all one word," she supplied.

"In a case like this, we usually start looking at the people who are closest to the victim. Husbands, boyfriends, or anyone who came into intimate contact. If those people check out, then we widen the circle."

The thought sat heavy on A.J.'s chest.

"Did you have a fight with anyone in the past couple of days?" Sheriff Justice continued down the line of questioning.

"Yeah. I've argued with someone in the last week."

The sheriff perked up. "And who was that?"

"A.J. McGannon," Tess replied.

5

"And what did you fight about?"

A.J. issued a sharp sigh as Tess stepped away from him.

"You can't be serious, Sheriff," he stated.

"I'm doing my job, A.J.," she warned. "I'm good at what I do for a reason and that's because I close every loop."

Tess felt bad mentioning their argument, but she'd been honest. "I've been asking him to cut down a tree that hangs over one of my buildings. It's too close to my property line and now I'm having foundation issues."

"We talked about this. You shouldn't have built that building so close to the fence anyway. The tree was there first and—"

He seemed to stop himself.

"He was the one who found me. I don't know if I'd be alive right now if he hadn't. There's no way he would've tried to hurt me and then been the one to come to my rescue," Tess stated before the argument got out of hand. She didn't want to frustrate the person who'd been so kind to her. "It doesn't make any sense."

"What were you doing on this side of the property this morning?" the sheriff asked anyway.

Tess steadied herself in case A.J. picked that moment to blow.

He didn't, though. He kept his casual and calm demeanor—the same stance that usually infuriated her when they were going toe-to-toe.

"I was riding fences like I do almost every morning this time of year." He was calm as a person could be when he responded and especially considering the implication was that he somehow had something to do with the crime committed against her. "I volunteer to check the area near the creek because that's where I found Bear almost three years ago, and we stop by for old time's sake. It reminds me to be grateful for the unexpected things that just show up in life."

Tess had never seen this softer side to A.J., a side that had him rescuing dogs *and people*. She couldn't afford to soften her stance toward him. She didn't *want* to care for any McGannon.

Of course, she couldn't go down that path with anyone and especially not someone she'd been fighting with for so long she forgot how many years had passed. It was strange, though, to realize just how much of a good heart A.J. had.

Normally, guys as good-looking as him ended up more stuck on themselves than anything else. She'd tried to pin that label on him, as well as on the other McGannons. Heck, each one looked like he could walk right off the pages of a magazine. But no matter how hard she tried, the label didn't stick. Each one was honest and considerate, and those were traits that fell in short supply.

A.J. was the best looking of the bunch, in her opinion, and that was saying a lot, considering the genes in that family. There was something special about those hazel and brown eyes of his that could be disarming. Which was exactly why she needed to remind herself to armor up around him. She wouldn't put it past him to use that chiseled jaw and just enough stubble to be sexy face to get his way in an argument.

Now that she was spending time with him under different circumstances, she realized there was so much more to him than she'd ever given him credit for. And that made him so much more dangerous to her.

It was strange, she realized, to live right next to someone for her entire life and truly know so little about them other than the basics. She was beginning to see there was so much more to A.J. than met the eye, and that her tunnel vision when it came to him had caused her to miss out on all of the good.

"Thank you, A.J., for cooperating," the sheriff finally said, and Tess could've sworn she felt him exhale a long, slow breath.

She would've made certain that he wasn't classified as a suspect. The words caused another shiver. Everything had happened so fast she was barely beginning to process. She couldn't even imagine what her father would say or think when he found out.

It was probably nothing, but she'd been even more concerned about him lately. His memory was slipping and that wasn't like him at all.

She would have to find a way to accept the fact her father wasn't the young man she'd grown up around. He was getting older and that was half the reason she'd worked herself to the bone around the ranch. He wouldn't agree to hire help if she asked because he didn't realize how much he was letting slip through the cracks.

"I'd been thinking about giving up my volunteer work lately. The ranch has been keeping me so busy it's hard to make time for the center," she said to the sheriff.

"Has anyone there been the cause of concern for you or threatened your personal safety?" the sheriff asked.

"We don't turn anyone away who needs help and my degree in social work allows me to council a variety of people. I doubt anyone there knows where I live, Sheriff." Tess loved her work at the center. She felt like she made a real impact there.

"You have a degree in social work?" The shock in

A.J.'s tone caused her to laugh, breaking some of the tension.

"Yes. I'm realizing there's a lot we don't know about each other." Tess bit back a yawn. Exhaustion was wearing thin and she wanted to take a hot shower. Her stomach picked that moment to growl, reminding her she hadn't eaten in...days.

Noises came from the direction where they'd come an hour or so ago and it didn't take long for Tuck to come into view. He was accompanied by a handful of deputies.

"If you guys are good here, I'd like to take Tess back to the ranch to eat and rest. She's been through an ordeal." A.J. must've read her mind. Then again, he was standing right behind her and probably heard her stomach growl.

"You know the way out," the sheriff confirmed.

"I do." A.J. shook a few hands, including Tuck's, on the way back to the trail leading to the ATVs.

Without saying anything else, he got them back to the big house in what felt like record time.

"Could I borrow the shower?" Tess asked as they walked back inside the house through the back porch. She noticed a line of boots in perfect order as A.J. added his to the collection.

She kicked off her shoes, and then followed him inside.

"You can have anything you want." Those words were tempting.

"I have a request that might sound a little strange," she hedged, not wanting to be alone in the big house.

"Oh yeah? What's that?"

"Could you stay in the bedroom while I have a proper shower?"

He grunted, and she was pretty certain she heard him say something about not needing the image of her naked in his head.

It should have offended her, but the comment made her smile. She liked the fact she was having an effect on him. Because being close to him made her pulse do things she hadn't felt in years and maybe never to this degree.

THE LAST THING A.J. needed was the image of Tess Clemente naked in the guestroom shower stamped in his thoughts. But he wouldn't deny her request, so he sat on the edge of the bed while he listened to the water running in the shower.

Control wasn't normally something he wrestled with and yet there he was wishing he could be under that showerhead with her.

Well now, that really made him crack up. The thought that he'd want to be in the same room with Tess, let alone naked, wasn't something he thought would ever occur to him. Getting to know her was definitely changing his opinion about her, but what did that mean exactly?

Hell if he knew. He was still trying to get over the fact he wanted to see her in a different light at all. It was probably just his protective instincts kicking in that had him off-kilter.

The spigot turned off in the next room and he prepared to see her walk out in a towel. Thankfully, she entered the room ten minutes later in a warm-up suit that he'd laid out for her on the counter.

"Thank you," she said almost immediately.

It was good that she spoke because he'd become fixated on a water droplet that was running down her neck, needing to trace the water trail with his tongue. He chuckled at himself because he was certain that move would get him slapped.

"You would've done the same." It was true. The ranching community might have their differences, but anyone would step in and offer assistance to someone in need.

A.J. stood.

"I need to figure out a proper thank you for Bear, too." The vulnerability in her voice was sexy.

"He'd be good with a head scratch and a bone." A.J. turned to head toward the kitchen but her hand on his arm stopped him.

"This is probably going to sound crazy coming from me, but I'd like to kiss you." Before he could mount an argument—believe him when he said that might take a while—she pressed up to her tiptoes and feathered her lips against his. Her thick silky lips against his sent his pulse into overdrive. The peck only lasted a few seconds but left a trail of damage in its wake. She opened her eyes and locked onto his gaze. He turned his body toward hers and then looped his arms around her waist as she closed the gap between them, her body flush with his.

Her full breasts pressed against his chest. He took in a deep breath, fearing they both were caught up in the moment and might regret these next actions later. But right now, he couldn't care about that. All he could focus on were her sweet lips that were still a little chapped. He liked the rough feel of them against his own.

She brought her hands up to his chest, and her fingers began outlining his muscles. Her fingertips left a heated trail.

A.J. dipped his head and captured her mouth, swallowing the moan of pleasure she issued.

Suddenly, her hands were on his shoulders and her fingernails were digging into his skin as she pulled him toward her. There was no room in between their bodies as it was, but she somehow managed to close what little gap that might have been left.

Body-to-body, he could feel her breathing against him, air coming out in rasps. Her pulse matched the tempo of his as it skyrocketed toward the sun.

She parted her lips and he deepened the kiss. She

tasted like peppermint toothpaste, which was now his favorite flavor.

The air in the room around them charged with electrical impulse and suddenly the fact there was a bed right next to them entered his mind. Considering this kiss had the kind of passion that had been lacking in all the ones that had come before it and he didn't want to take advantage of the circumstances, he pulled back.

Looking into her glittery eyes didn't help matters. If this was down to primal need and she wanted proof of life he'd happily oblige in consensual, no-strings-attached sex.

But something down deep warned him this would be so much more than that. Having sex with Tess would be a game-changer.

She practically panted against his lips and that didn't help him with what he needed to say next.

"We should get some food in you."

She nodded but there didn't seem to be much conviction there.

Taking a minute to catch his breath, he finally clasped their hands together and asked if she was ready.

Again, she nodded, and he wasn't sure if it was a good sign that she seemed to lose her ability to speak. That wasn't normally a problem for Tess. She generally had more words than he wanted to hear, but he could admit to stoking the flame every once in a while, just for fun.

There was something about the passion in her voice when she was furious that made him smile. Passion was missing in most people. She had it in spades. And it was one of her more attractive traits. Of course, he didn't always see it that way when he was on the wrong side of a dispute with her but in this light, it was damn sexy.

By the time they returned to the kitchen and fixed her a plate of leftover enchiladas that Miss Penny had made, the back door opened, and the sheriff filed in. The look on her face said she had news.

A.J. fixed himself a cup of coffee while the sheriff finished up a call. He returned to the table about the same time she ended the conversation. He offered coffee, which she quickly no-thank-you-ed. Not a good sign.

Her expression was set and there wasn't a smile for miles around on her stone face as she clasped her hands together.

"You might want to sit down, Tess." The sheriff's tone fired up all A.J.'s warning signals.

Tess complied.

"We got an immediate hit on the crime scene the second I filed a report." The sheriff's gaze had been steady on her own hands. She looked up at Tess when she said, "This isn't his first time to strike. A victim was found in Round Rock last week."

Round Rock was a city just north of Austin that the Dell Computer Company had put on the map. It was largely responsible for the suburban sprawl that it was today.

"The victim was believed to have been abducted from outside her residence. She was taken into the woods on the outskirts of town where she was kept in a hut made from tree branches and stones." The sheriff held eye contact with Tess like she needed to make sure it was okay to keep going. "There was a pile of leaves circling the hut, just like here."

"Did she make it out before he..." It was like Tess couldn't say the rest of the words out loud.

The sheriff shook her head. "She was hanged to death before being cut down and then covered in leaves up to her neck."

6

"Now that we have more than one victim, that shifts our focus."

There was some measure of relief that the sheriff was no longer looking at the people closest to Tess. "What does that mean exactly?"

"We'll still interview your staff and everyone on the McGannon ranch, but we're going to be widening our view of what kind of criminal mind we're searching for." The sheriff seemed to choose her words carefully.

"Meaning?"

"We'll be looking at how the two of you might be linked. Social circles or touchpoints through your work or alumni associations," Sheriff Justice explained.

A.J. brought over a plate of finger foods and Tess absently started nibbling. It was good to have something to keep her hands busy more than anything else. Next, he brought over a pad of paper and a pen.

His cell buzzed and he checked the screen. "Tuck is out front, and I just got a text from Hawk that he's on his way. I'll move them in through the front door and set Tuck up in the formal living room. It's far enough down the hall to give him some privacy and it sounds like the tone of the investigation has shifted. You're looking for witnesses at this point."

The sheriff nodded. "I just got a message from one of my deputies. Tess's phone is nowhere to be found near her barn."

"If my ranch hands saw anything, they wouldn't sit on that kind of information, but it never hurts to ask," he informed before disappearing down the hallway. Hers were used to her disappearing a couple days at a time.

Nerves were getting the best of Tess and she noticed it even more after A.J. left. The tether to him was keeping her grounded in the craziness of this case. Her brain was still trying to sort out everything that had happened, and she hated thinking of anyone she knew as a possible suspect. She couldn't imagine anyone who would actually want to hurt her, let alone kill her. She also drew a blank on anyone who could be fixated on her.

That creepy-crawly feeling settled over her again, causing her body to shiver.

The absence of A.J. in the room had a physical effect on her. The realization shocked her beyond words. She blamed it on biology. There was something about his presence that had a calming effect on her. Which was weird because he also sent her pulse racing and made her heart pound her ribs. She got a light, almost giddy feeling in her belly that had a strange way of righting the mixed-up and crazy world.

And the kiss they'd shared—the one that had been meant to be a peck on the lips—held more heat than she'd ever experienced. She'd never had a kiss before that could *curl her toes,* but she finally understood the expression.

Since all of that was too much to process while she was dealing with the fact someone had just tried to kill her, she stuffed her emotions down deep and refocused.

A.J. returned and took a seat next to her. "Tell us exactly what happened in Round Rock."

The sheriff nodded.

"The victim was reported missing two weeks ago by her husband when he got a call from his mother saying his wife never came to pick up their daughter. His mother had been babysitting so the victim could run errands and do some shopping for the little girl's birthday. She was turning one year old the following weekend and they were hosting a birthday party for her." The sheriff double-checked her phone screen, where she must have had bullet points on the crime.

"I'm not a mother, so our profile doesn't look like a match."

"No. In the Round Rock case, the victim was taken

from her home. Her vehicle was in the garage and the door was still open."

"She was bringing in a load of supplies." Tess's statement was met with a nod.

"None of her neighbors reported seeing anything unusual. So, the perp most likely would have been driving a vehicle that could blend in," the sheriff supplied.

"Do you mean like a service-oriented vehicle?" A.J. asked.

"That's right. A fake cable company or delivery van. Any of those would disappear in a suburban neighborhood." She checked her phone again. "There were no cameras in the area. This neighborhood had always been deemed safe. There were lots of families."

Kids and family neighborhoods, minivans. Those were things that hadn't been on Tess's radar. She'd pretty much given up having a social life to take on more responsibility around the ranch, but there was more to it than that. Her last couple of relationships had ended badly.

Tess's childhood had been fortunate but there was another word that came to mind. Lonely. She'd learned the ranch business and focused on her studies. She'd had a lot of friends at school, so she'd always had someone to talk to in the halls, but her overprotective father had kept a strict curfew that pretty much ensured she'd get through high school without ever attending a party.

Her friends had stopped inviting her after being told no a dozen times. She'd entertained herself by reading and spending time with her menagerie of animals. Occasionally, she was given permission for a girlfriend to sleep over, but her life was boring to her teenage friends who were into sneaking out and boys.

Tess liked boys, too. She was too chicken to sneak out and, besides, living out on a massive ranch made it difficult to go anywhere. The Rapunzel jokes had gotten old even though she'd been too stubborn to let her friends know how much the comments had offended her. She'd kept that to herself and had gotten really good at stuffing down hurt.

Being tough on the outside had helped her avoid confrontation. She almost laughed at the thought, wondering if A.J. would see it the same way.

"Austin PD interviewed her husband and family members. The victim was a devoted mother and wife. She worked part-time from home with her own party planning business that she'd started from the ground up. The vendors she worked with all thought highly of her and her mother-in-law adored her. She paid her bills on time. No one seemed to hold a grudge against her, and the case has already gone cold." The sheriff made a tsk noise. "Such a sad situation."

"The woman who was murdered." She paused for a second letting that last word sink in. "Can you tell me her name?"

"Aurora McKnight."

Tess searched her memory for an Aurora and came up empty. She wanted more than anything for that name to resonate. "I'm sorry."

A.J. LISTENED, trying to draw his own conclusion about how these two cases might be linked. As far as he could tell, there wasn't much to work with. Aurora McKnight was a work-from-home mother with a young daughter and husband. The family lived in Round Rock. The city was north of Austin and Tess made a routine trek through there to volunteer every other week.

"Do you ever stop off in Round Rock?" he asked Tess.

"I'm sure I have for gas, but it wasn't a usual routine." Her gaze shot up and to the right, like it usually did when she was recalling facts. It was also a sign she was telling the truth but then again, there was no reason for her to lie.

"No favorite coffee shop or breakfast spot?" Austin and its surrounding area had so many little spots for foodies. It wasn't uncommon for a popular place to have a long line and an hours-long wait. People did it, too. They'd stand in line for everything from donuts to barbecue to tacos if the food was worth it.

A.J. preferred cooking on the grill at home. Some of his happiest childhood memories happened outside at this ranch with his brothers and cousins. His father had built a baseball diamond out back after seeing Ryan throw a pitch. A.J.'s brother eventually turned down a shot at the minors saying he loved the backyard games better. Cattle ranching was in Ryan's blood as much as it was in A.J.'s, their brothers and cousins.

"No. Not in Round Rock. I have a few favorite taco stands in Austin but I'm usually up at the crack of dawn to make the drive and then home long after sunset. I'm never too concerned about stopping along the way. I drive straight through unless I make a gas stop."

Information was so easy to access these days, it wouldn't be difficult for someone who'd developed a fixation to get personal details about a target based on something as simple as a gas stop.

"Do you have any identifying features on your personal vehicle?" The sheriff seemed to be thinking along the same lines as A.J.

"Yes. Clemente Cattle is on everything we drive, including personal vehicles. My car has the ranch's logo and bumper sticker on it," Tess supplied.

"What does the victim look like?" A.J. asked.

"Blond hair. She was petite, coming in at five-foot-one. She had blue eyes." The sheriff read the details from her screen.

So, basically, nothing like Tess who was tall at five-feet-seven-inches with chestnut hair that was thick,

long and silky. Her neck was long and dignified, like a
dancer's. And her eyes were the color of honey.

His thoughts drifted to how she'd felt in his arms
and the heat in the kiss they'd shared. He couldn't
afford to let that happen again. Helping Tess in the
vein of being neighborly and building goodwill in the
ranching community was one thing. Getting involved
with her as anything else couldn't happen.

"I wish I could help." The frustration in Tess's voice
also revealed how tired she must be. She'd been
through an ordeal and as soon as this interview was
over, he planned to see if he could convince her to rest.
At least she'd been nibbling at the plate of food he'd
brought over.

The sheriff asked a few more routine-sounding
questions about Tess's habits.

A.J.'s cell buzzed. He glanced at the screen and then
the sheriff. "Hawk has the guys lined up to speak with
you when you're ready."

"Thank you, A.J." At least he seemed to be off the
sheriff's suspect list. "I'm ready now unless Tess has
any other questions."

"No, ma'am." Tess bit back a yawn.

"Then you'll want to follow me." A.J. led the sheriff
into the office his father sometimes used. The main
office was in the barn, but Clive McGannon lived his
work and wanted to have access to his files and a quiet
place to work whether he was inside the big house or
in the barn.

There was a line in the hallway. A.J. acknowledged each person before shaking Hawk's extended hand. There were lots of wide eyes and curiosity that A.J. wished he could address but figured the sheriff wouldn't approve. She would want to question everyone first. Then he'd be allowed to share more information, once everyone was cleared of course.

When he returned to the kitchen, the plate of food was empty, and Tess had laid her head on the table. He didn't want to interrupt her, but it was getting late and she, like most ranchers, were usually in bed early. Work on a cattle ranch started around four a.m. most days.

He walked over, not wanting to startle her if she'd actually gone to sleep and placed a hand on her shoulder.

"I'm awake." She brought her head up. "Every time I close my eyes, I see that place."

"How about going into the guestroom while all these interviews take place?" he offered, figuring at some point her spunky self would return and she'd tell him no just to argue. Guilt nailed him at the thought. She'd been nothing but sweet and there was no reason to think that would change.

The new Tess was going to take some getting used to.

"Okay. Would it be too much trouble to ask for another glass of water?" She pushed to standing and he could see the move took some effort.

"Not at all." He couldn't feel worse for the circumstances, but he liked seeing this side to Tess. She allowed him to see her vulnerability. Most folks mistook being vulnerable for being weak. A.J. believed the opposite was true. It took a lot of courage to be vulnerable to someone else. Breaking down walls wasn't easy and especially not for someone who'd experienced a tremendous amount of pain.

Until getting to know her recently, he'd believed she'd lived a charmed life. He and his brothers had nicknamed her *princess* because of it. Man, had that whole image been shattered into a thousand tiny pieces in the past fifteen hours.

His entire impression of her had been so far off base he needed to start over.

After pouring another glass of water and offering an arm, he guided her down the hallway and toward the guest suite. Never mind that her warm and moist lips had been pressed to his mouth in this same room a few hours ago.

He killed those unproductive thoughts because they had his heart pounding his chest like he was a teenager on a prom date. He'd never been around someone who could pull out all his strengths and insecurities at the same time.

Tess stopped at the threshold of the bedroom.

"What happened in here before...bad idea." She quickly added, "Not that it wasn't great, I mean, it was pretty amazing."

"You think I'm amazing?" If he could reel those words back in, he would.

That made her smile and her cheeks turned five shades of red before she managed a response. "I was trying to protect your feelings, A.J."

Ouch.

"It's just the timing is off and we usually..." she seemed to search for the right words, "...rub each other the wrong way."

"Well, now you've gone and put another image in my head," he teased but he was only half joking. Wasn't there always a hint of truth in every joke?

"You know what I mean." More of that embarrassment showed and it was so damn sexy that he needed to focus on something else. Fast.

"I'm just giving you a hard time, Tess. This might surprise you to hear coming from me, but I'd actually like to be friends. There's nothing great about what you've been through these past few days. So don't get me wrong, talking and trusting each other is something I hope we can build on." His heart seemed to want something else, but he needed it to be reasonable.

Putting him and Tess together was like pouring gasoline on a fire most of the time. The fact they were working well together now showed their maturity in being able to put disagreements behind them when the situation dictated it.

They should be proud of how far they'd come and their willingness to build on this truce.

"I have to say, A.J., it's been nice for me, too." Those words shouldn't score a direct hit in the center of his chest. She was only agreeing with him.

"Good. We can go from here."

7
———

T ess's bones hurt. Exhaustion had settled in. She couldn't have done more than doze off in the last couple of days. She wanted to tell A.J. about the special *thing* happening to her when it came to him, but she doubted she'd be able to express herself very clearly.

The bed called. Her body answered. All she could think about was curling up underneath the covers and praying those images of the hut in the woods wouldn't keep her awake, haunting her.

"I'll grab a laptop and work in the chair over here while you go to sleep, if it'll make you feel more comfortable. Being in a strange house might make it hard to sleep."

She appreciated his consideration and he was right on some level, the McGannon home should feel strange. Except that it didn't. Being here with A.J. felt like the most natural thing.

It must be lack of sleep causing her mind to grab hold of delusional thoughts. She'd dated men whom she'd viewed as safe for the past few years, not willing to risk her heart only to have it broken again. What had made her so protective? Was there even one event? Or was it a culmination of a life that had been wrapped in a protective coating?

For as long as Tess could remember, she'd been discouraged from taking risks. Watching the lifelong heartache her dad had experienced at her mother's snub had left an impression. And then there'd been Cole Winthrop, the TA in her English class at University of Texas at Austin.

A grad student, he'd been in his twenties when she'd been a sophomore. Lit had been her favorite subject. He'd handed her a graded essay with a small piece of paper clipped to it that had his number scribbled on it.

He'd always carried a leather-bound journal with things he'd observed, and his poetry written in it. He came from a wealthy Houston family who owned and operated an authentic French restaurant. The south of France was where they'd spent summers.

Tess had grown up around the quiet types, men who held their feelings so tightly to their chests they'd rather take a burning gas bath than talk about them.

She'd been around the strong, silent type her entire life.

Cole had been the exact opposite. He'd keep her up late at night talking Tolstoy and Kafka. Cole liked to talk whereas her father spent evenings in front of his laptop catching up on ranch paperwork. He'd have a cold beer after a long day's work. Football season was the only time a TV was on and he caught all the Sunday games.

Tess had been certain that Cole hadn't watched a sport in his life. He was an intellectual and spent his days debating ideas. The trouble was, he liked winning arguments a little too much. And even though the relationship was starting to run its course, she'd been devastated when she found out he'd been 'studying' with four other coeds.

When she'd confronted him about the others, he'd shrugged his shoulders like it was nothing and told her that he didn't remember ever saying the two of them were exclusive. Not exactly the words she wanted to hear coming from the man she'd given her virginity to.

Her lack of experience had shown, too. She'd thrown a fit and a couple of notebooks at him on the lawn of the clock tower where he was splayed out on a blanket with a picnic basket complete with wine and cheese.

The worse part was that she'd lapped up every one of his practiced lines about her being special and the only one he could *really* talk to. Clearly, he was *talking* to plenty of others. The whole *feeling isolated from the world* bit had worked on quite a few young coeds.

Looking back, she couldn't help but wonder if she'd had a *sucker* sticker on her forehead or if Cole was just that good at picking out the loners in a room. Once she'd gotten past the humiliation of the relationship, she'd closed off a piece of herself to everyone else since.

Strangely, she felt a draw toward A.J. that made her want to open up to him a little more. Test the waters. See if she could trust him.

He had a lot of experience and she'd dated around quite a bit since those early days, too. Still, no one had stirred her heart or made her feel like she could go all-in since...

When she really thought about it, maybe never. Her relationship with Cole had been puppy love, not the real, lasting kind. Then again, it wasn't like she had a whole lot of examples to draw on there.

Her father had quietly dated around. He'd spent time away from the house and especially once Tess was old enough to take care of herself.

In fact, she had a sneaky suspicion her father was dating someone seriously in Dallas. His visits had become more frequent and he stayed longer each time. He came back looking pretty wrung out and she needed to have a talk with him about this double life he'd been leading. The one that made him even more drained than being out in the sun all day. Although, he did that, too.

They needed to have a heart-to-heart. She was just past her thirtieth birthday and found it strange that her and her father's lives were so different, despite living under the same roof. At least, she thought his life was different. He'd been so secretive, and she understood in the beginning that he probably didn't want to discuss anything in its early stages.

Did he think she wouldn't be happy for him?

He never discussed her mother or their relationship but over the years Tess had realized that it gave him great sadness. The two had never discussed her having a boyfriend and she sure couldn't talk to him about Cole.

She'd been close with one of her nannies, but Helen had been shipped back to England when her two-year work visa had expired. Helen had been the last one. Tess was tired of meeting someone new every two years. She'd decided at sixteen that she could take care of herself.

Having so much responsibility for the ranch while growing up had caused Tess to grow up fast in so many ways. Just not when it came to relationships or guys. Those lessons had come the hard way—good old-fashioned heartbreak.

She tried to close her eyes, but the image of the hut descended on her with the weight of a heavy blanket. She blinked her eyes open and looked at A.J. on the sly.

It was nice having a McGannon on her side for a change.

"You doing okay?" he asked, startling her.

"Sorry. I didn't realize..." She thought better of finishing that sentence. As it was, her cheeks were on fire from being caught staring at him.

"It's all right." The way he chuckled to himself as he closed his laptop sent a trill of electricity shooting through her. "Do you want to talk about it?"

"NOT REALLY." Tess pushed up to sitting and then fluffed up the pillow behind her. "I'd like to talk about something else, *anything* else, because it's all I can think about."

The look he gave said he understood whole-heartedly.

"We've been neighbors our entire lives and yet I feel like I've learned more about you in the past fifteen hours than in thirty years. How is that even possible?" Her question was spot on with what he'd been thinking throughout the day.

"We ran in different circles in school. Plus, I was a few grades ahead of you," he supplied by way of explanation.

"Three grades," she said proudly.

"That sounds about right." He chuckled to himself.

"You were popular, A.J."

"Really? Interesting. I never really saw that in myself. I had my brothers and cousins—"

"Who were all like the most popular kids in school," she added.

"I don't mean to sound shell-shocked, but I don't think we saw it that way. We were a tightknit bunch and—"

"And you guys mastered pretty much every sports team there is," she said.

"We showed up with a family big enough to cover every position in nearly every sport." That much was true and having grown up on the ranch, all the McGannons were athletic. Sports came naturally to them and they enjoyed playing ball with each other.

"What about you?" He turned the tables. "What did you like about school?"

"Lit class." She shrugged. "My friends."

"I don't remember seeing you much outside of school," he admitted.

"My dad was pretty protective; after my mom left, it was just the two of us." She paused and ran her finger along the blanket. "Don't get me wrong, I had a great childhood. There was always food on the table and decent clothes on our backs. It was just the two of us and whichever nanny or au pair could get a two-year visa. There was a revolving door, which made it hard to get close. I always knew they'd leave, and we'd lose touch no matter how much they promised otherwise."

"Some of the best parts of my childhood was

knowing my family had my back. It must have been difficult to get close to a person only to have them leave."

She confirmed with a nod, and he could see that she was doing her best to put on a poker face.

"I never was clear what happened with your mom," he said.

"That makes two of us," she admitted. "She left one day when I was a little baby, and never came back. My dad never talks about her and I stopped asking questions when I saw how much it hurt him."

"Must be strange to have family out there, somewhere, and not know who they are or if they're okay."

"When your mom makes the decision to walk out of your life when you're not old enough to take care of yourself, their welfare isn't the first thing that comes to mind." Her point was fair.

"Have you tried to locate her?"

"No. Why would I?" The defensiveness in her tone was a warning of the amount of pain the topic seemed to bring.

So, he decided to tread lightly. And it was probably because he was coming from a place where he'd give his right arm for one more day with his mother. Every situation was different, and he acknowledged that not every mother deserved the love and respect his did.

"I'm not taking her side, so I hope you'll take this comment in the spirit it's meant. I'd want to hear her side of the story. I'm probably just a stubborn mule, though." He tried to laugh it off, but Tess stared down at the piece of blanket she was working in between her fingers.

"Honestly, I've just been so mad at her that I never really thought about it from that perspective." She slowly looked up at him and his heart took another hit when he saw that rare vulnerability in her eyes. It said that her mother was one of the few people who could actually hurt Tess.

It made him want to protect her more than anything.

"It's worth considering. You might get answers from her that you can't get from your father," he said.

"I'm half expecting him to come back from Dallas with someone on his arm. Or an announcement that he's walking away from the ranch. Although, I can't honestly imagine him not living and working Clemente Cattle."

"What makes you think he's seeing someone?"

"His trips are longer and he's wearing himself out trying to go back and forth as much as he is. I keep warning him to slow down but talk about stubborn. My dad invented the word."

A.J. could relate there. He'd grown up in the business and it took a pretty stubborn person to make a cattle ranch profitable. His family owned mineral rights to the land they lived on, and that's where their fortune had come from. He suspected it was the same for the Clementes.

But cattle ranching was their legacy. Once it got in the blood, any other job would feel like settling.

"Thanks for talking to me about my mom, though." She circled the conversation around. "My dad never talks about her and she's just been this big void in my life. It's strange to think the person who gave birth to you could be out there somewhere. I don't even know who she is or if I'd recognize her if we passed each other in the street. For whatever reason, I decided a long time ago that she would've moved to Austin."

"It seems like everyone has for the past decade or so." The saying, *Keep Austin Weird,* was born out of so many corporations moving in that folks were afraid the town would lose its charm. Chain restaurants started popping up. Residents delayed infrastructure in the fool-hearted belief they could keep people out if there weren't enough roads. The only thing their stance did was glut up traffic, A.J. mused.

He also wondered if her mother was the reason Tess made the trek every other week to volunteer. She could have helped in the community of Cattle Cove. No town was perfect, and they'd had more than their fair share of crime in recent months.

There were needs in the community she could have addressed rather than drive all the way to Austin. Speaking of which, "Can I ask why you volunteer at the particular center you chose? I mean, why not somewhere close by? That's a long drive."

"It is. That's true." She shrugged. "I fell in love with

Austin when I was a student there. If I'd had my way, I probably would've stayed as a social worker. I was struck by how much homelessness is there and I wanted to make an impact. I started volunteering at the center while I was local."

"Have you been volunteering there all this time?" he asked.

"I quit for a few years and then I got a call out of the blue. I guess I shouldn't have been too surprised. I'd talked my dad into making annual donations, but they were always on behalf of the ranch and not me personally. I never really told anyone there what I did for a living. One of the people I'd worked with became the director and put two-and-two together. Eloise contacted me and explained how short-staffed they'd been. She remembered what I was getting my degree in and asked if I could help."

"To which you agreed." Making that drive and for no reason other than to help someone worse off than she was cut through more chinks in his armor. A.J. was doing a real bad job of keeping his guard up around her.

At least they hadn't kissed again. They'd been smart enough to keep from going down that path despite having the urge.

"I wanted to help. There's no better feeling than knowing you made an impact in someone else's life." Her words were spoken with such passion.

"It's the noblest thing a person can do." He couldn't

help but wonder if her need to give healing to others had to do with lacking it for herself.

"Wow. Thank you, A.J. Don't take this the wrong way, but I didn't think you'd understand." Her honesty made him laugh out loud.

"I'm not the jerk you must've thought I was," he said in his own defense.

"No. You're not a lot of things I thought before. I'm glad that I've had a chance to get to know you better." She looked at him with honey brown eyes that glittered with need.

And he was in trouble.

8

"I should probably try to sleep." Tess had yawned three times in the last two minutes. Bear was already snoring. Someone had given him a shower and she suspected A.J. had arranged it with Hawk.

"I'll stay right here," A.J. reassured, repositioning his laptop before checking his phone.

"Everything okay?" she asked as he seemed to study a text.

"Yeah. It's just my brothers and cousins checking in. We do our best to talk every day even if it's only by text."

Talking with A.J. had lifted burdens she'd been carrying for years. His suggestion to locate her mother had resonated with her.

It was highly possible that the woman never wanted to see or hear from Tess again. She could put herself on the line and get rejected, but there was only one way to find out for certain. Rather than spend the rest of her life wondering, she could track her mother down and ask. There were so many tools available now that would make a person easy to locate.

In a strange way, she'd always held the belief that wanting to find her mother was somehow betraying her father. The last thing she wanted to do was hurt the man who'd cared for her when her own mother had walked away. Her father might have hired nannies to bring her up and his priority had always been the ranch, but at least he'd had the decency to stick around.

Tess had no doubt the man loved her in his own way. He might not have been a doting father, but he was consistent. She had no doubt in her mind that he loved her. He'd spent long days building up the family business he wanted to hand over to her someday. In a strange way, she realized it was how her father showed his love. He wanted her to be financially sound long after he was gone. The legacy business he'd built would belong to her at some point.

Tess settled in underneath the blanket, liking the weight of it on her. Before she realized, she fell asleep.

It was still dark outside when Tess opened her eyes again and she had no idea how much time had passed. She woke to the click-click-click sounds of fingers on a keyboard and looked up to find A.J. studying the screen in front of him.

She didn't stir and he didn't seem to notice her watching him this time. Her heart, on the other hand, freefell in her chest at the sight of him.

After a few selfish minutes, she stretched her arms out and made a show of yawning.

"Good morning." A.J.'s voice had an early morning raspy sound that sent warmth spiraling through Tess. He immediately set his laptop down and picked up his coffee mug. "I was just about to go for a refill. Do you want anything while I'm up?"

"How about bacon, eggs, and toast?" she teased.

"Done."

"Hold on, I was just kidding." She motioned toward his coffee cup. "I'd love one of those, though."

He nodded before walking out of the room. By the time he returned, she'd washed her face and brushed her teeth.

True to form, he brought in a breakfast casserole, that smelled like heaven, on a tray with fruit and a cup of coffee.

"Thank you. I was just kidding but this smells amazing." Tess was beginning to feel half human again. The clock read four-thirty a.m., her usual time to get up and get going. In all the excitement of yesterday, she'd forgotten to sit down with her ranch foreman.

"I can't take credit. Miss Penny keeps the fridge stocked. In fairness, all I had to do was hit a few buttons on the microwave." He set the tray down on the bed next to her.

"Remind me to thank her the next time I see her. And I'll thank you now for pulling it all together and bringing it to me. I'm pretty certain this is the first time I've been served breakfast in bed without having a fever." She laughed and it felt good to break up some of the tension.

He scooted the chair next to the bed and took a sip of coffee. Bear whined in his sleep but seemed to soothe himself quickly.

"What's on the agenda today?" he asked.

Noises sounded, coming down the hall. Voices. There were two, a male and a female. One belonged to Miss Penny and the other was Tess's dad.

Instinctively, Tess pulled the covers up to her chin. It was strange to feel like she was a teenager getting busted for sneaking a boy in her room. And when she really thought about it, she lowered the covers and climbed off the bed.

No doubt, her dad was worried sick. The second he entered the room, she was struck by just how much.

"I'm okay, Daddy."

"How could you be?" Her father looked like he'd aged ten years in a week. He marched over to her without acknowledging A.J. or Bear, despite the dog's low growls, and wrapped his arms around her.

All the driving back and forth seemed to be taking

a toll on his weight. It seemed like he'd dropped even more pounds since she'd last seen him.

"Seriously, Dad. It all worked out." She tried to reassure him but he didn't seem to be having it. He held her so tight she could feel his bones.

"I shouldn't be away so much." His self-reproach made her feel even worse.

"I'm thirty years old, Dad. I'm a grown woman. It's not reasonable for you to be around me all the time and, guess what, it's okay." She did her best to reassure him. His brow was furrowed and there were deep grooves in his forehead from age and worry. His skin had a yellow tone she hadn't realized before. Then again, despite living under the same roof—albeit on a large estate—the two had mostly communicated via e-mail. Text was his weakness, but the man could fire off e-mails. He was normally up and out before she started her day, a habit he'd started last year.

"Not good enough. If I'd been home—"

"This still might have happened. It's not your fault." Her reassurances seemed to fall on deaf ears.

He took her hand before glancing around with a look of disgust. "Let's get out of here."

"Oh. Dad." She was almost speechless. "Have you officially met my friend, A.J.?"

"Since when have you been friends with a McGannon?" Her dad's face puckered like a prune.

"I'm A.J., sir." A.J. stepped forward with an outstretched hand.

Her father just looked at it and didn't make a move.

"Dad, that's rude," she said under her breath. Embarrassment heated her cheeks. She thought her dad would have more consideration. "He saved my life."

A.J. got the biggest grin on his face. He smiled ear-to-ear. She told herself to ask him about it later, once she got her dad to act civilized.

"How much do I owe you?" Dad had no plans to lighten up.

Rather than stand there and watch as he insulted her friend, she said, "Go on home. I'll be there in a little while. I need to talk to A.J. alone."

"There's no reason for you to be here any longer. I'm back." Her father seemed determined to dig his heels in. She'd allowed his overprotective nature to rule too long. It was time to stand up for herself.

"I'm not trying to hurt your feelings, but I already said I'd be home soon. Someone needs to talk to the foreman and ranch hands since they all had to be interviewed yesterday. Why don't you handle the ranch and I'll be home when I can?" She used as calm a voice as she could muster. Had she really let her father run her life before? It hadn't felt like it, but then she hadn't really ever challenged him like this before now.

Tess had long been wanting to talk to her father about hiring help to run the ranch. She'd been putting off the conversation because she knew exactly how it would go. Her father was stubborn. Knowing him, he'd volunteer to step in and do more. She'd been working crazy hours to avoid an argument.

The workload was too much for one person. She needed help and he couldn't do everything.

"Why can't you come home now?" This time, he used his hurt voice and it usually worked. She was starting to see it for the manipulation tactic it was and, as much as she loved her father, giving in would only cause her to lose ground.

Working the ranch wasn't something she'd ever wanted. Her heart had been in social work. Her father had given her permission for the degree, but he'd made a strong case for her to come home and work beside him.

It had taken a life-threatening situation for her to realize she'd been allowing her father to control her life.

She took his hand and walked him to the front door, stopping at the threshold. The sneaky grin on his face that said he believed he was about to get his way lit a fire inside her.

"I'll meet you at home in a couple of hours. I have a few things to take care of first. If I need you in between now and then, I'll call on your cell." Come to think of it, he was handy with every other piece of technology. Why hadn't he mastered using the cell phone? He was one of the smartest people she knew. He'd be able to figure out how to perform basic functions. And even if he couldn't, phones made everything so easy. Literally, he could use voice commands to hear his text messages and perform a host of tasks.

He started to protest so she stopped him with a question.

"Where have *you* been?" she asked.

"Hold on now. Don't turn this conversation around, missy."

"Excuse me?" She hadn't been called that name since childhood.

"You and A.J. McGannon had been nothing but hostile toward each other. Or have you been keeping your friendship secret for a reason?" Well, that really torqued her.

Taking in a deep breath to calm herself, she touched his arm.

"Dad. There's no one I respect more than you, so I hope you'll trust that I know what I'm doing." Appealing to his softer side seemed to be working. "But as far as keeping secrets goes. Who are you seeing in Dallas? You can trust me. I'm not going to give anything away. You can date whoever you want. It's none of my business. Just like my friends are none of yours. Common courtesy says—"

"To hell with that common courtesy nonsense." His tone was sharp. It was time to end the conversation before things got out of hand and someone said something they'd regret.

"Okay, Dad. You're tired. You've driven a long way and you probably need to get some rest." She stood there a little dumbfounded when he turned around and stomped off.

A.J. DRAINED his cup of coffee and set the mug down. He decided to check on Tess even though he knew she was a grown woman, more capable of handling herself and anyone else for that matter. Though her father had seemed determined to give her a hard time and A.J. found himself wanting to ask Tess what was going on with that.

She came bouncing in the room.

"Don't get me wrong. He's my dad and I love him, but that man can be infuriatingly stubborn." She blew out a breath and paced across the floor.

"How long has he been sick?"

Tess spun around with the most heartbreaking look of shock. "What?"

"He's lost a lot of weight since I last saw him. I'm guessing it's because he has some kind of illness."

"That would be news to me," she countered.

"I'm sorry." A.J. hadn't meant to be the one to surprise her with the information. It was plain to see that he had, though.

She whirled around and sat on the edge of the bed. It looked like her mind was racing. "I just accused him of going to Dallas to date. I thought it was stupid of him to hide that from me. It doesn't matter to me who he goes out with or where she lives."

"I didn't mean to be the one to tell you," he said.

"I'm certainly glad you did. The funny thing is that I saw him losing weight and it registered. But sickness? It didn't cross my mind." She seemed to be going down a blame game. He hoped to shed some light on why it might not have registered.

"You see him every day. I don't. It was more of a drastic change from six months ago when I last ran into him," he reasoned.

She rocked her head.

"There's something else." He didn't want to drop another bomb on her. Not saying anything didn't seem like fair play, either. So, he went ahead with it. "He's wearing makeup. I'm guessing it's to give him more coloring."

Tess slapped her hand against her knee. "I missed all the signs."

"It's easy to do when you see someone every day."

Her shoulders sank forward. "I would have been nicer to him."

"There's nothing wrong with standing your ground, Tess."

"He's sick. So many things make sense to me now. A few months ago, he stopped eating breakfast at the same time as me. He's been going in and out of Dallas so much that I thought he was dating someone there. It was probably a doctor." She sat, dumbfounded.

"To be fair, he didn't want you to know."

"That makes it so much worse to me."

"Why is that? I understand a father wanting to protect his only daughter." A.J. didn't have kids and part of him wasn't so sure he ever would, but if he had a daughter someday, he'd want to protect her from the world.

Tess slid off the bed onto the carpet next to Bear. She absently stroked his fur. Chin to chest, A.J. was almost certain a few tears fell but he gave her privacy and didn't ask.

After a few minutes, she tilted her head up. Her eyes were just as beautiful.

"I wish he had enough confidence in me to know that I can handle anything he throws my way. He has spent most of his life overprotecting me. I'm guessing that's a hard habit to break. Living his way instead of the life I want doesn't seem so appealing to me anymore." She turned her head and locked gazes. "I never really set out to run a cattle ranch."

"Then why do it?" A.J. loved his work and couldn't imagine doing anything else, but cattle ranching wasn't for everyone.

"For him. I didn't want to disappoint him."

"I'm not taking the man's side. Believe me. But maybe in his own way he's doing the same thing for you." A.J. didn't care much for Mr. Clemente but that didn't stop him from wanting Tess to understand her father's point of view. He was talking it through for her sake, not her father's.

Bear lifted his head, stretched and then cozied up to her even more. Lucky dog.

"Maybe we could figure it out better if we actually talked about something important for a change. He's never been built that way. He had a tendency to steamroll over me when I bring up an important subject. You saw for yourself how he acted when I said I'd be home in a little while."

"I'm not saying it was good." A.J. had no idea why she'd insisted on sticking around. He liked it and his heart had given a little flip at the thought she wasn't ready to go home. They'd come a long way in a short time. If they could change, he had to think it was possible for her father to see the light.

"Besides, do people ever really change?"

"I'd like to think we're a perfect example of the possibilities." He heard the defensiveness in his own voice.

"But are we?"

The fact she would question him after everything he'd done for her sent fire through his veins. Was he overreacting? Yeah, probably. But he said the next words anyway.

"Then why are you still here?"

"I was just asking myself the same question." Tess got up and silently left the room.

9

Once his temper cooled, A.J. realized he'd made a mess out of the situation with his knee-jerk reaction. It wasn't like him to wear his emotions on his sleeve. Tess had always known how to push his buttons and yet he didn't think that had been her intention this time. In fact, she seemed scared and vulnerable.

Damn.

Since she needed a friend more than he needed his pride, he took off jogging down the long hallway with Bear at this side. Maybe it wasn't too late to apologize.

When he ran past the living room, he stopped and did a double take. There she sat, looking lost and alone. His heart would never recover from the sight.

"So, here's the thing. I don't have a purse or cell phone. I have no money on me. My dad's already gone, and, if I'm honest, he's not the person I want to talk to right now." She didn't look up. Instead, she stared at a spot on the floor.

"Okay. Tess..." A.J. searched for the right words. He was bad with apologies and he wasn't even sure why he felt the need to say he was sorry anyway. "I just wanted to let you know that you're welcome here anytime. And, getting to know you better has been—"

"Interesting?" Her eyebrow shot up and she risked a glance at him.

"Great, actually."

"I don't have any of this figured out. All I can say is that being around you makes me feel..." her gaze darted around before she came out with the word, "calmer."

He'd take it.

"Then, why don't you stick around for a while today. We can figure out our next move together," he offered.

"Sounds like a good plan to me. I'd like to head down to Austin at some point. I missed my day at the center and it's not like me to disappear like that. The director will be worried. She might have been reaching out all this time on my cell and I wouldn't know it. Plus, the case might make news, especially once the press links the two cases."

"They might have already," he said.

"My patients will need to see that I'm okay. A few of them can't afford setbacks, A.J."

He had the fleeting thought one of them might be

responsible for her abduction but that didn't make sense considering she wasn't the only one who'd been targeted. Still, there had to be some link.

"I'll grab my laptop and see what else we can find about Aurora McKnight," A.J. said.

Tess brightened at the suggestion and he liked being the one to make her feel better. He liked that she was getting more comfortable with him. And he liked that they'd actually been able to talk through a disagreement instead of ending on a heated note.

This was progress. He'd take it. His heart wanted to make an even bigger deal out of it but he shut that down before it could take off.

A.J. returned with the laptop and joined Tess on the sofa where he took a seat next to her. He opened the laptop and placed it on the coffee table. They both scooted toward it and their outer thighs ended up touching.

A jolt of electricity vibrated up his leg and went straight to the center of his chest. He'd move his leg if he didn't like the damn feeling so much. It reminded him that he was alive after having what had felt like the same date with multiple women far too long. He saw that it was possible to get *more* from a relationship, to *feel* more than casual about someone.

He refocused on the laptop screen and pulled up the article about Aurora McKnight. He skimmed the details and waited for a reaction from Tess.

"The article basically tells us what we already

know," she said with more than a hint of disappointment in her tone.

"Yes. Sheriff Justice gave us most of these details. I was hoping something might spark but it's okay if it doesn't."

Her body language was closed up and tense.

"He's done this, or at least tried, to two women now," she said. "I can't help but think he's not done."

"The attacks were weeks apart. One in Round Rock and now Cattle Cove. The cities don't have much in common," he stated.

Tess issued a sharp breath. "The other thing that bothers me is that he made it onto Clemente property without being seen. Our operation isn't anywhere near as big as yours but that feels like a bold move."

"He took the other victim in broad daylight," he added. "One similarity is that you were both at home when the abductions occurred."

"True. The perp took both of us out in the woods. The article says the other victim wasn't sexually assaulted. I know I wasn't, either. There were no signs of her being beaten or tortured. Same for me. Although, he didn't get very far with me before I escaped, so I don't know what his intentions were," she admitted on a sharp sigh as if reliving the details made it hard to breathe.

Seeing her reaction was a gut punch.

"The crimes look ritualistic." A.J. took note of the details in the hopes a pattern would emerge that could help unlock the identity of the perp. "The perp had to have built the huts ahead of time. The noose was ready to go. So, the whole scene in the woods had to have been created beforehand. Both of his targets have been taken from their homes."

"So, he had to have been watching us and studying our habits for a while," she said.

"His crimes seem premeditated. Someone who is that systematic with creating a crime scene wouldn't likely pick someone at random. His victims would be chosen carefully." Anger shot through him at the thought someone had been stalking her. Granted, he and Tess had spent the better part of a decade squabbling over everything from fence lines to who was responsible for clearing dead leaves that fell from trees whose limbs extended onto her property. She'd gotten on his last nerve more times than he could count. But he didn't wish her any harm.

"How do we stop him from doing this to someone else? There's almost endless wildlife areas and ranches between here and Austin. This guy could be in Houston by now or have headed to North Texas." They needed to find a link between Tess and Aurora.

"I need to get a message to my father and let him know we're taking a trip to Austin." She was right. There wasn't anything else to see in Cattle Cove.

Going back to the crime scene in the woods would only bring back horrific memories. Besides, the sheriff and her deputies had worked over the area and he didn't want to infringe on an active crime scene.

"Did you happen to notice if the reporter mentioned what the perp used to bind Aurora's hands?" she asked.

A.J. pulled the article back up and scoured it.

"Bingo." He looked up at her. "He used baling twine."

"Then we know whoever this bastard is he had access to twine."

Tess walked toward A.J.'s truck. Bear had been right by her side until he seemed to realize where they were headed. He came to a dead stop.

"What's wrong?" she asked A.J. The weary look in Bear's eyes nearly stopped her heart. All she wanted to do was drop down beside him and wrap her arms around his neck, make him believe everything was all right.

A.J. was locked onto his dog so much so that she doubted he'd even heard her question. "You're okay, buddy. You know I would never do that to you."

He made a kissing noise, turned and confidently walked away.

"You're good, boy. You got this." A.J. opened the passenger door and then walked around to the driver's side. "I got you."

She could've sworn she heard Bear heave a sigh before he galloped toward the truck and then hopped onto the floorboard before finding a spot to curl up on the bench seat.

"That's right." A.J. showered his dog with attention and love. "You did it."

Bear looked like he was smiling while being doted on.

Tess climbed in beside him and shut the door.

"Everything okay?" she asked.

"It is and it always will be. Bear's figuring it out, too." A.J. started the engine and pulled down the drive.

"Why is he like that?" she asked.

"The best I can figure is someone must've driven him out here and dumped him. When I found him at the creek, he'd been surviving on his own for a while."

"That's cruel. Everyone should know a domesticated animal won't survive for long in an environment he's not used to. Even a big guy like him could be taken down by a multitude of wild animals." Fire licked through her veins as she thought about Bear scared and alone in the woods.

"He wasn't in the best of shape when I found him, but he survived and I promised him that he'd never have to be alone again." Those words scored a direct hit with Tess.

She tucked her chin to her chest to hide her watery eyes while she got her emotions in check.

She made a silent promise to check on Bear once in

a while after this whole ordeal was over. She needed him to know people would stick around.

"He's lucky to have found you." She meant every word.

"That's what you would think. Turns out, it's the other way around." A.J. chuckled to himself. She might not understand the private joke going on but her admiration for A.J. hit dangerously high levels. Dangerous for her heart. She tried to blame it on the fact that she'd have a helluva time coming at him with a hard line in the future now that she'd seen this side to him. She needed to maintain a safe distance to stay objective.

But the truth was that she couldn't *unknow* the fact he was a really great person. Anyone who was kind to animals had a special place in her heart. Rather than go too far down that road, she refocused on the case.

Tess chewed on the information about the twine on the road to Austin. Logic said he might have bought the twine off the internet. It was the same blue color they used at Clemente Cattle and A.J. had said his family's ranch used it, too.

So, basically, it was widely available and probably used on half the ranches in Texas if not more. It didn't exactly narrow down their search. She filed the information away anyway because it could prove useful later.

Tess leaned back in the seat. Bear had positioned himself comfortably in between her and A.J., and

Bear's head was presently resting in Tess's lap. She scratched him behind the ears thinking how true it was that pets lowered the blood pressure of their owners.

It didn't hurt matters that he'd saved her life, but Bear had wedged his way into her heart. She was going to have to ask A.J. if it was possible for her to stop by just for visitation with his dog.

A.J. had plugged the center's address into his GPS. Tech made life a whole lot easier to get around in strange cities, but she could drive this route with her eyes closed.

Traffic in Austin slowed considerably, starting in Round Rock. She remembered stopping off at a gas station on her way out of town a couple of times and wanted to swing by to talk to the clerk. It was such a long shot that the person working behind the counter would remember her, but she was desperate and willing to try pretty much anything.

It couldn't hurt to ask about regulars or see if the convenience store attached sold twine by chance. She tried to pull any other details out that might help. Thinking back, had she stopped off for a soda on her way home any place other than the gas station?

Tess didn't think so. She couldn't be one hundred percent certain that she'd *never* made a pit stop, but none came to mind. She also tried to think about anyone she'd come into contact with who might want to hurt her.

The thought was seriously creepy. She'd been working with several unstable men at the center, men who were battling various addictions. There were others who had mental health issues and no insurance. The door was open to everyone and there were days where the line for services and aid looped around the block.

Eloise, the director, was a saint for taking on the top spot. She was a good person and was probably worried. It was a good thing that Tess was making a personal visit. A few graduates of the program had been offered jobs at the center. There was Bryan Harker, Rhett Daniels, and Joseph Waylon. Bryan did general office assisting. He ran errands and deliveries. Rhett had been given a job as janitor after successfully receiving treatment. He'd taken over for Bryan who'd parlayed his janitor job at the center into a late-night stocking position at a grocery store.

But if she was talking about nature, her mind snapped back to Rhett. He was a twenty-nine-year-old who'd been through the wringer. He described his walks in the woods as cheap therapy. But then, most people who lived in Austin liked the outdoors.

There were more interesting hiking spots in and around the capitol than she could ever conquer if she had free time for a year. If Rhett knew what was going on, he'd be worried about her, too. He didn't like the fact she drove so far, every time she came to work at the center.

A.J. maneuvered onto Fifth Street and, miracle of miracles, found parking on the same block as the center.

"Have you thought about playing the lottery today?" she teased, needing to lighten the mood from her heavier thoughts on the way over.

"Downtown parking must be my thing." He cut off the engine and put a leash on Bear.

"You probably just wasted all your luck on finding this spot."

"I don't know, I might be able to score us a couple of the best tacos in Austin, ending the great debate over Taco Deli or Torchy's once and for all." Now, he was delirious.

"I'm not sure I want to know who you think should wear that particular crown." She climbed out of the truck and then shot him a warning look. "Your answer could drive a wedge in our newfound friendship."

"Not you, too," was all he said as he shook his head.

"What does that mean?"

"I don't eat out much, but I can't say with the utmost sincerity that I've ever eaten a bad taco," he clarified.

"Good. Because if you'd picked a side, we might have to part ways." She smiled and started the short walk toward the center.

As usual, the line was longer than hours in a day.

"This place always so busy?" A.J. asked.

"Afraid so. There's a lot of need here. It's one of the

things I like best about my work. I'm able to help so
many people and from so many walks of life. Of
course, I can't mention names, but I've helped treat
everyone from once-country and western legends to
homeless veterans who served our country. Everyone is
treated as equals and we have some of the best services
in Austin." She issued a sharp sigh. "On bad days I
would tell you we barely make a dent in the need for
our services."

"Can I say that I respect you even more now?" His
words were spoken with the kind of reverence that sent
warmth spiraling through her.

"That's a compliment I'll take, McGannon." Tess
maneuvered them around to the back entrance to navi-
gate away from the line.

"Is it wrong that I'm concerned about the number
and types of people who have to be turned away every
day?" His point was valid, and one she'd considered.

"Not really. I've had those thoughts myself. I've ran
through pretty much every scenario I can think of in
my mind on the drive," she said.

"Is that why you were so quiet?" He took her hand
in his and linked their fingers.

She'd be lying if she said it felt anything but good
to be physically connected to A.J. In fact, good was
probably too tame a word for the way her heart danced
in her chest every time he was this close.

They stopped long enough for Bear to do a little
business in the back alley. A.J. unhooked the leash to

give his dog some leeway and Bear immediately moved to a small patch of grass next to the building, which pretty much left A.J. and Tess standing toe-to-toe.

"It would be a really bad idea to kiss you right now, wouldn't it?" she asked.

"The worst of bad ideas," he agreed with one of those devastatingly handsome grins.

But looking into those hazel-brown eyes, she got lost in the moment and in the feeling of his hand in hers—his was rough from working on the ranch. She liked the feel of it.

Then there was the days' worth of stubble on his chin. Instead of making him look sloppy, which would be damn difficult to do on a face as attractive as his, it somehow added to his charm.

In that moment, she wanted nothing more than to feel that roughness against her skin. She wanted to feel the friction burns on her cheek. She wanted to feel alive.

So, she did the one thing she wasn't supposed to. She kissed him.

A.J. groaned against her lips as he looped his arms around her waist. He pulled back enough to say, "I was hoping you'd do this."

And that was pretty much all the encouragement she needed to dive deeper into that bad decision. It didn't help that there was so much heat in the kiss it suddenly felt like she was standing on rubber bands instead of legs.

That bone-melting feeling traveled all over her body, leaving a scorching trail in its wake and pooling between her thighs. Not one man had made her feel so many sensations with so little touch before A.J.

She tried to convince herself that the chemistry between them came from a whole lot of years of tangling over property lines and disputes over water. But that would be a lie.

The simple truth was that A.J. McGannon was hotness times a hundred. He was the real deal. Perfect body. Check. A face that women would literally line up to see. Check. A real person behind the gorgeous face. Double Check. Intelligence. Check.

The checks were racking up and she was just getting started.

He also threatened to open spaces in her that she knew she wasn't ready to shed light on. So, basically, it was going to suck when she had to go back to arguing over moving a tree away from her equipment building before the foundation cracked.

10

A.J. needed to power down the attraction that was fast becoming a runaway train. But with her lips pressed to his, it was damn difficult to think rationally.

He pulled back enough to rest his forehead on hers. He needed to catch his breath before they went inside and, based on her chest heaving in rhythm with his, she needed the same.

The devil of the situation was that they were neighbors. If she'd been a random person who lived in town, he could deal with dating and the inevitable breakup. He rarely ever went into town so interaction would be at a minimum.

Getting involved with Tess Clemente was basically shooting himself in the foot. They didn't get along on a good day. Of course, that was before. Now, they'd established a tentative line of trust.

And what was he doing? Messing it up by kissing her. Technically, she'd kissed him, but he'd welcomed the move and who'd initiated it was beside the point anyway. Then there was that nagging voice in the back of his mind that kept telling him that he could *really* like Tess.

That was probably worse than not liking her, which he'd almost made a profession out of doing for the last decade. She'd become a bigger and bigger thorn in his side. Make her mad and he figured he hadn't even seen the tip of the iceberg yet when it came to the trouble she could cause him.

He didn't want it to matter that he hadn't shared a kiss that intense in longer than he cared to remember. Making her laugh genuinely made his day.

Of course, her father hated him even more now despite the fact A.J. had literally saved the man's daughter's life. But then, Clementes and McGannons had been gasoline and fire for years. Getting along would take some practice and a whole lot of work. Plus, there were all the ridiculous Romeo and Juliet jokes he'd have to endure from his brothers and cousins.

Nothing was worth giving them that kind of material to work with.

Not even a kiss like...okay. He stopped himself right there. Maybe the kiss would be worth it.

Standing there, breathing in Tess's jasmine and citrus scent, made A.J. blindly believe all the issues between them and reasons the two of them were a bad idea could be overcome and, somehow, magically everything would work out. Since that was about as practical as driving a tractor from Texas to Vermont, he shoved those unproductive thoughts aside.

When their breathing returned to a reasonable rate again, A.J. put Bear's leash back on. "Ready to head inside?"

"Ready as I'll ever be." The flush to Tess's cheeks caused his heart to take another hit. Much more of this and there'd be no recovering.

He linked their fingers and followed her inside the back door. The center had a row of offices, five on each side, with walls made of Plexiglas. The implication was privacy without being isolated. He was reminded of the possible dangers of doing this kind of volunteer work.

A.J. believed he'd seen a deputy's vehicle out front and realized he was right when he heard a familiar voice. Tuck. It made sense that he was here doing the same thing they were, drumming up leads and investigating.

A woman who looked to be close in age with Tess came bolting toward her, bringing her into a hug the second she got in range.

When they broke apart, Tess introduced the woman as Eloise Gates.

"No relation, by the way," Eloise said, referring to her famous last name. She shook A.J.'s outstretched hand as he supplied his name.

Her eyes lit up in the way everyone's did when they found out he was a McGannon. His last name was associated with one of the biggest fortunes in Texas, and that was saying a whole lot.

He also had plans to pitch an idea to add Austin-Cares to their charity list to his brothers and cousins, along with his father when he woke. A.J. couldn't allow himself to believe any other outcome was possible for his father.

Clive McGannon had to wake from his coma. Period.

"It's so nice to meet you," Eloise wasn't wearing a band, so he took her flirting to mean exactly how it came across.

"Ma'am." That one word usually shut down those thoughts in the opposite sex.

Tess cleared her throat, obviously not thrilled with her boss.

"Your father called. He said you might be stopping by today," Eloise said. She was a couple of inches shorter than Tess. Five feet, five inches, if he had to guess. Most men would probably consider her attractive. Her hair was blond with a blue streak, which was fashionable. She had blue eyes and a heart-shaped face.

She paled in comparison to Tess, in his opinion. But Eloise was good looking.

"He explained why you've been out. I'm so sorry that happened to you." Eloise looked to be almost in tears. She seemed genuine and her concern was real. "First with Aurora and now you."

Tess's forehead wrinkled. "Hold on a minute. Did you know Aurora McKnight?"

"She used to work here. Don't you remem—" She froze and then it looked like the answer dawned on her. "Aurora was here before you came back. And her last name was Parks. She quit when she got married and her last name changed to McKnight."

"Aurora worked *here*?" Tess echoed. The shock seemed to hit her at the same time it struck A.J.

The connection between victims was the center.

"Yes. But it's been a while since she left," Eloise supplied. "And now this happened to you."

"How long as she been gone?" A.J. interrupted.

"Three or four years."

"Do you keep the same clientele or do people cycle in and out?" he continued. A picture was emerging.

"Most people cycle in and out. Our goal is for people not to need us long-term," Eloise supplied. "Some of our clients move away and then we help others find more permanent services and support. We're a crisis center and we like to get our clients out of crisis mode."

"Would any of your clients have known both Aurora and Tess? Is it possible someone stayed around that long?" he pressed. This was the closest they'd been to getting real answers and he could feel a breakthrough was close.

"Well, yeah. There's one." Eloise turned to Tess. "You know who I'm talking about, don't you?"

"I do, but there's no way." The wounded look on Tess's face made A.J. want to reach out to her and pull her closer.

The front door opened, and Tuck walked in. A.J. waved the deputy over.

"Rhett Daniels has been at the center for over seven years," Eloise supplied. "He used to be in the program before we offered him a job as a janitor."

"I know Rhett. He wouldn't..."

Tuck was making his way toward the trio who were still standing in front of the offices. He introduced himself and after names were exchanged and he was brought up to speed, he said, "Mind if I take a look at Rhett's office?"

"Not at all," Eloise said. "Follow me."

She led them to an area that had a small break room. There were bathrooms and then a closet. The final door housed Rhett's office.

Eloise tried the handle and all it did was click. "This door isn't supposed to be locked."

She pulled out a keyring with a dozen keys on it, trying one after the other until she found the magic one. She inserted it and then twisted the knob. The door opened and she flipped on the light.

Stepping inside the small space, A.J. fisted his hands at his sides.

Tess gasped. Her mind was still reeling from the realization that her father had been hiding a mystery illness from her and now, walking into Rhett's office, she was immersed in tree limbs and leaves.

The place was neat, a little too neat actually, but that wasn't surprising given Rhett's obsessive nature. And it was no surprise that he loved being outdoors. Camping was his favorite thing in the world to do.

The extent of the decorations in his office was alarming given the context of someone being killed and an attempt having been made on Tess's life. Wouldn't she somehow know if it had been Rhett?

The short answer was no. She didn't get a look at her attacker. The blow from behind had come out of the blue. She hadn't heard him until he'd been right on her. Of course, it didn't help that she kept a wireless earbud in her right ear that had disappeared along with her cell.

The word, *ritual,* came to mind. The perp who could now be referred to as a killer had a ritual that involved nature. Every muscle in Tess's body pulled taught. A sharp pain between her shoulder blades plagued her.

She tightened her grip on A.J.'s hand. This startling development caused her stomach to cramp and nausea to slam into her. She had been one of Rhett's counselors and biggest champions.

Tuck took the lead, and everyone backed against the wall to make room for him to walk through. Having four of them plus Bear inside the small office was body-to-body tight. Tess also noticed that Eloise positioned herself on the other side of A.J. The director practically glued her body to him.

Tess rolled her eyes so hard they could've gotten stuck. Tucking the bout of jealousy down deep, she immediately searched behind her for Rhett. He wasn't there. And he would be bothered by the fact so many people were inside his tidy office. He'd be afraid someone would touch something or move an object a hair out of place.

His anxiety would be through the roof. Whoever killed Aurora and made the attempt on Tess was a sick individual. Only a mentally twisted person could do what he'd done to another human being and then target someone else.

"There are pictures of both victims with Mr. Daniels on his desk," Tuck informed. He turned around and made eye contact with Tess. "I need to call this in to the sheriff." He paused. "Before I do that, I need to speak to Mr. Daniels."

Tess led the way, backing out of Rhett's office. A small crowd had gathered in the hallway.

"Nothing's going on. You can go back to what you were doing before," Eloise said, shooing them away. She stopped in front of A.J. and blushed. "You can wait in my office if you'd be more comfortable."

"I'm good. Thanks, though," he quickly said, not giving her any encouragement and yet Tess still burned.

It shouldn't surprise her that her boss's face would flush every time she looked at A.J. Tess certainly had no claim on the man even if her heart reminded her of the passion in those few kisses they'd shared. It was probably because their lips had been locked less than half an hour ago behind the building and not because her feelings for A.J. were spiraling out of control.

Tess searched for Rhett through the crowd of people. He should have been right up at the front but wasn't anywhere to be seen.

Eloise was doing the same thing as she pulled out her cell phone. She fired off a text and surveyed the faces once again.

Tuck, who'd taken out his phone and started snapping pics before Tess had gotten out of the small office, emerged. "Has anyone located Mr. Daniels?"

This was so not good for Rhett.

A.J. shook his head and turned toward Eloise. "If I could use your office to speak to Tess alone, I'd appreciate it."

Eloise nodded as she made a phone call to Rhett.

"Lead the way." A.J.'s voice was low and quiet as he bent down and whispered in her ear.

As Tess walked away from her director, she heard her leaving a voicemail for the janitor, telling him to contact her immediately.

Once inside Eloise's office and with the door securely shut, Tess said, "Don't ask me why, but I just don't think Rhett is capable of something like this."

A.J. sat on the edge of the large oak desk and tugged Tess toward him. She leaned into him and he looped his arms around her. Bear sat next to A.J.'s leg, looking like he wasn't thrilled with all the activity.

"The evidence against him isn't looking good," he said.

"Wouldn't this all be classified as circumstantial, though?" She should be looking for reasons for Rhett to be guilty instead of innocent, but for some reason she just couldn't bring herself to believe it.

"This is probably enough to get a warrant to search his home. If Austin PD finds anything there the evidence could stack up. But, yeah, I do think what we've found so far is circumstantial," he agreed. "What makes you think he's innocent?"

"Rhett has always liked the outdoors. We've always known that. He never has made a secret out of it. His favorite activity is camping. He goes almost every time he has a day off. So, the fact that his office has an outdoor theme doesn't really surprise me all that much." There were outdoor living magazines neatly stacked on his desk and color coded. He had a kerosene lamp sitting on top of his filing cabinet.

"Which also makes him fit the profile on a basic level," A.J. said.

"I know you're right and if I didn't know Rhett, I might think the exact same thing about him."

"Your familiarity with him might be causing your opinion to be biased," he pointed out.

"That's true. But it also means that I know him and in my heart of hearts I don't believe he's capable."

11

To A.J.'s thinking, Tess couldn't afford to be naïve when it came to Rhett. Before he could dig deeper into his argument as to why, Tuck knocked and then opened the door. "Rhett Daniels took off. Texted his boss that he decided to take time off and go camping," he said. "There isn't much else you two can do here while Austin PD looks for him. Thought you might want to head home."

A.J. looked to Tess, hoping she would agree. He couldn't get her out of there fast enough as far as he was concerned.

Tess bit her bottom lip, a sign she was contemplating what he said. Her gaze bounced from Tuck to Bear. "It would be good to get him out of here. And I do need to have a conversation with my father."

"Is that a yes?" A.J. asked.

She nodded. "Let's get Bear out of here."

In A.J.'s mind, Rhett was the most likely candidate, and it wasn't because the law thought so. The fact that the abductor seemed obsessed with nature and that he covered his victim with leaves gave him the impression the killer cared about his victims. He was covering them, almost as if he were tucking them in.

The hanging part was still a question mark, but answers would most likely come in time as the investigation unfolded.

Tess started toward the door and then stopped. She looked directly at Tuck. "Is there any chance I can go with the officers who search Rhett's home?"

"Absolutely not." Tuck left no room for doubt in his tone.

She put a hand up. "I'm mainly offering because I'm concerned about his mental state when he sees strangers going through his personal belongings."

"Austin PD already has a team heading to the site. They're a cooperative agency. If they find anything at Mr. Daniels, they'll let us know. If he shows up there, they'll bring him in for questioning," Tuck supplied.

"Something like this could set him back. He's been doing so well. His life has changed in the past couple of years," she argued.

Tuck softened his expression. "In my experience, innocent people don't run."

Hearing those words seemed to take a physical toll on Tess. She clamped her mouth closed and nodded.

A.J. walked her out to the truck in back and, after

giving Bear a minute to make sure he was good for the long ride home, took the driver's seat.

Tess blew out a sharp breath and pinched the bridge of her nose. "I probably sound crazy defending Rhett."

"Evidence does seem to be pointing in his direction." He paused as he navigated onto the highway. "Believing in someone despite the odds makes you hopeful though, not crazy."

"Between this and thinking about something being wrong with my father...which reminds me, I need to call my half-brother, Hudson, and see if he knows anything about our father."

A.J. couldn't get past the words, *half-brother.* "Whoa. Hold on a second. What do you mean by your half-brother?"

"Oh, right. I guess no one really knows about him. Hudson Leonard is his name. He owns a successful logistics business in Galveston, and he lives near Houston. His mom asked for full custody, I guess. I'm not very clear on the details and, I think we've already figured out that my father is a big fan of keeping me in the dark when it comes to anything important or involving family."

"He didn't take your father's last name?" A.J. was surprised. The Clemente name would open a lot of doors for Hudson. Then again, A.J. understood the urge to spread his own wings and make his mark on the world without the hand-up a well-known name would provide.

Being a McGannon could be both a blessing and a curse. Considering he worked from sun up to sun down most days, he didn't have a whole lot of time to worry about which.

"No. I guess not. I have no idea why. He just showed up one day and Dad introduced Hudson as family. Dad said that I had a brother and should treat him like family. I don't remember much before the age of ten, but I clearly remember being seven when that bomb was dropped."

"I take it the two of you aren't best of friends." Stranger things had happened, but A.J. was still a little bit shocked by this news.

"We talk every once in a while. He usually calls during business hours and it often feels like a work call to be honest. I don't know that much about his mother and it always felt a little awkward to ask. He and Dad talk once a month or so. When my dad was first pulling his disappearing acts, I thought he might be meeting up with Hudson," she admitted. "Now we know how off base I was."

"Would your father tell Hudson the news about being sick?" A.J.'s family mostly knew each other's business. They checked in every day and everyone had been keeping close watch on the family patriarch.

"I seriously doubt it. They talk and are cordial but, believe it or not, I'm closer to my dad than Hudson is.

He only visited a handful of times over the years, but I always thought it was nice of him to check in with me. At least he made an effort," she said.

Family was important to every McGannon. Everyone lived their lives and especially as they were all grown men, but he couldn't imagine anyone holding out on anything so important.

Tess settled back into her seat and absently stroked Bear's fur. A.J. liked how much she seemed attached to his best friend. She leaned her head back and closed her eyes for a bit as he made the rest of the drive.

"Where am I taking you?" he asked.

"Home, I guess." Why did those words feel like a gut punch? He'd seen her through a difficult experience. He'd stood by her side, so turning his blinker to indicate a right turn to her house instead of a left turn to his shouldn't be a problem.

The next fifteen minutes went by in dead silence. The Clemente home was a two-story colonial-style home with black shudders against white siding. The porch was long and there were several bright red rocking chairs lined up.

He pulled into her drive and then eventually in front of her house where the sheriff's vehicle was parked.

"What's she doing here?" Tess asked quietly but she wasn't looking for an answer.

"She might have an update," he said. "And, considering a crime happened on his property, she might be here to speak to your father."

"He wasn't here. I doubt he'd know anything." Tess turned to A.J. "Will you come inside with me?"

He wanted to say that he would. But then what? She needed to have a private conversation with her father. He'd be a third wheel.

Curiosity was getting the best of him as to why the sheriff was there but the thought of walking inside only to leave a few minutes later was a gut punch.

"I better head home," he said and the look of disappointment on her face almost made him change his mind.

Almost.

TESS HAD no response to A.J., so she scratched Bear behind the ears and climbed out of the truck. Before she closed the door, she stopped long enough to say, "Thank you, A.J. I can't imagine what would've happened if you two hadn't been checking fences and if you didn't like to revisit the spot where you found this good boy."

"If you need anything, or even just to talk to someone, here's my number." His voice, normally strong and steady, was low and sincere as he rattled off his contact information.

Daggers would've done less damage to her heart

than walking away from that truck as she committed the information to memory. It felt like she was walking away from her first real friend in longer than she could remember, and a voice deep inside her told her that she needed to fight a little harder for it.

His engine sat idling, so she turned around and walked right back to the passenger side. He rolled down the window and a look of concern creased his forehead.

"Everything all right?" he asked.

Words were failing her in the worst way, and she figured this might not come out perfectly, but she needed to say it. "Stay for dinner. Coffee. Something. Let me feed you. I just don't want to be alone right now."

Being back on her family's property should comfort her. Knowing her father was most likely sick and keeping it from her wasn't helping her feel more secure. What else was he lying about or covering?

Facing him was going to be difficult. *He* could be a difficult man. But she felt a renewed compassion toward her father now that she understood what might be going on. The possibility that he could be very sick didn't help her melancholy mood.

Without a word, A.J. put the gearshift in park and cut off the engine.

"Coffee sounds good," he said as he came around the driver's side.

"I feel like a broken record right now but thank you

for coming inside." She wanted him to know how much she appreciated him for it.

He fell in step beside her and reclaimed her hand. She was pretty certain that he said something about being in trouble. The words were so low she strained to hear them. Bear happily accompanied them. Her father had a strict rule about no animals in the house, but she figured now that he knew Bear had saved her life there'd be an exception.

Stepping inside the house, the air changed. It was heavier than she realized and only part of it had to do with the voices coming from the kitchen.

"I'm home," Tess shouted so she wouldn't surprise the sheriff and her father. "And I have company."

She walked in first and her dad's gaze could've melted a glacier when he saw who trailed behind her. To his credit, he didn't say a word. Not even when Bear trotted across the man's precious travertine flooring.

Now, she was starting to believe in miracles.

Tess immediately moved to a cabinet and pulled out a large bowl that she filled with water. She grabbed a dishtowel and set up Bear's water dish next to the back door. He splashed and water flew around the bowl. Again, her dad practiced enormous restraint. She saw the strain on his face.

"Sheriff," A.J. said as he walked over to the island where she sat.

"I was planning to call the two of you but figured

stopping by in person might be for the best," she said after a greeting.

The sheriff sure knew how to get Tess's full attention. She moved to the island and took a seat.

"Rhett Daniels hasn't come back home or to work," she started. "Austin PD is keeping an eye on his apartment and place of business. Did he mention his favorite camping spots to you during any of your conversations or sessions?"

"What will happen to him?"

"Tess. I'd rather you answer my question first," Sheriff Justice stated. "I know how fond you are of Mr. Daniels and we're doing our best to keep an open mind, despite evidence that leads us toward his guilt."

"What did you find in his apartment?" Sounding defensive wasn't going to help Tess's case. So, she rolled her neck to work out some of the kinks and tried again. "Believe me when I say that I want whoever's responsible for Aurora's death and my..." She couldn't bring herself to say the words in front of her father with how distressed he looked. "So, don't take this the wrong way but I also feel like I know Rhett."

The sheriff was nodding but something was brewing behind her eyes. Something that made Tess think twice about continuing.

"There's a third victim," the sheriff supplied.

Tess got to her feet and moved to the coffee maker. She made quick work of brewing two cups, one for her and the other for A.J. as the sheriff gave details like location and name. Cindy Fairbanks was another volunteer counselor at AustinCares. She didn't have a social work degree, so she didn't work with cases like Rhett but the two would've known each other. "She's only twenty-three."

Tess was sick to her stomach.

"This is a list of items Austin PD found at the suspect's residence." The sheriff produced a piece of paper with handwritten notes. She set it on the granite island.

Tree limbs in various stages of staining

Tent set up in the living room

Leaves

Mod podge

Stain

Rope

Texas Wildlife magazines

Outdoor Camping magazines

Pictures of co-workers

"His entire apartment was filled with the kind of supplies used in the murders," the sheriff informed.

Tess folded her arms across her chest and tapped her foot on the tile. "Whoever did this is an animal. Cindy was one of the sweetest young people I've ever met. She worked at the center evenings after her job at the capitol. She worked as an aid for one of the senators. Cindy also volunteered at a soup kitchen two nights a week. She was one of the kindest people on the planet."

"Her roommate reported her missing when she didn't come home from work two nights in a row. That was almost a week ago," the sheriff supplied.

The doorbell rang and Tess looked to her father.

"I'm not expecting anyone," he said with a shrug.

12

As much as Tess didn't want to leave her father in the same room with A.J., she figured having the sheriff around would help keep the peace. "I'll be right back."

Whoever was at the door was impatient. The doorbell sounded before she was halfway down the hall and then the person knocked on the door to boot.

Tess swung the door open so hard she had to catch it before it smacked against the wall. "Hudson. What are you doing here?"

"I came to see if you were okay." Her half-brother charged into the house. He stopped short when his gaze caught on something behind her.

She turned to find A.J. standing there, practically taking up the entire doorway into the kitchen. His arms were folded, and he leaned casually against the wall but made no mistake about the fact he'd be right behind her in a heartbeat if she was threatened in any way.

Rather than marvel at what a nice surprise it was for someone to have her back for a change, she whirled around on Hudson. "Dad is in the kitchen with the sheriff."

"But you're fine?" There was so much concern in his voice.

She felt bad for snapping at him. He seemed genuinely concerned about her and his coming all the way here might be a little over the top when he could've just called...oh, right. Her cell was still missing.

"Yeah. I'm shaken up and pretty freaked out by the whole situation, but physically I'm fine," she said to him. "Do you want to follow me into the kitchen?"

"Okay." He stopped long enough to make a show of staring at A.J. "Who is that guy?"

"A.J. is a friend of mine. He's actually the one who found me."

"Well, then I need to shake his hand." He walked straight down the hallway and offered a handshake that A.J. took.

After brief introductions, Tess moved to the kitchen where her father and the sheriff were huddled over the list and her cell phone.

Her father looked up. "Nice of you to come, Hudson."

"Thanks for the text." He walked over and embraced their father.

Tess had questions. Like when did the two of them become so close that her father was texting Hudson during emergencies? Of course, the scary part was over, and it was really nice of her brother to drop everything and come all this way on short notice.

A.J.'s expression was stone when it came to meeting Hudson. She couldn't read his reaction one bit. And it was probably owing to the fact her emotions were on overdrive, but it was weird having Hudson there.

Of course, her father could pick this time to announce his health issue. The thought grounded her. What if something was seriously wrong with her father?

Despite his stubborn ways and the fact he could be suffocating, she couldn't love him any more than she did. She appreciated the sacrifices he'd made in bringing her up by himself. He'd been there for dinners and birthdays. He might not have been demonstrative with affection, but she knew in her heart that he loved her. She'd never once questioned his affection for her.

After Hudson was introduced to the sheriff, she packed up her items and then said, "If Rhett Daniels contacts you in any way, I'd appreciate a phone call."

The sheriff produced a business card and set it on the island.

"Will do, Sheriff," Tess confirmed.

"I hope this goes without saying, Tess, but if Rhett Daniels *does* reach out, I'd like you to use extreme caution. Call me. Let me do my job. If he's as innocent as you believe he is, the truth will come out. He'll be exonerated. But we can't clear him if we can't reach him, if we can't talk to him and get his side of the story. Find out where he's been the past few weeks."

Tess was rocking her head in agreement before the sheriff finished. With the body count rising, and Cindy Fairbanks as another victim, the killer had to be connected to the center in some way.

"I'll see the sheriff out," her dad said and then the pair of them left the room.

"Coffee maker is over there." Tess pointed for her half-brother.

"I'd rather have something stronger if you have it." He walked over to the fridge like he was right at home.

A.J.'s eyebrow shot up. But all Tess could focus on was the case.

Rhett would have to speak to police in Austin in order to clear his name. She hoped it wouldn't set him back emotionally. If he was innocent, there were resources available for him. He knew how to reach out. If he was guilty...

She didn't want to go there but she had to face facts. There was an alarming amount of evidence pointing to his guilt. If only she had her phone so she could check to see if he was trying to get a hold of her.

Maybe she could talk him into voluntarily going in for questioning.

Tess tucked her hair behind her ears. Suddenly, the walls of the house she'd grown up in were closing in around her. She moved to where Bear was lying down and sat beside him on the cold tile.

A.J. seemed to be assessing the situation as her father returned.

"I'm tired," he said, "I think I'll turn in early."

"Not so fast, Dad. We need to talk." She realized the stress of the day was probably a lot for him. It had been hell on her, too. But they couldn't keep sweeping everything under the rug and hoping it would go away.

"I've been brought up to speed by the sheriff. You're home safe." He seemed to be drawing a blank on what else there could be to discuss.

"How long have you been sick?" The question scored a direct hit.

"Who told you that?" His gaze didn't waiver, so she assumed this was news to Hudson, as well. He'd opened a beer and had taken a seat at the table.

"I have eyes. You've been more tired than usual for months. I thought you were secretly dating someone in Dallas, but it's not hard to put two-and-two together to realize you're going to a doctor or for some kind of treatment regimen."

He started to protest but she stopped him with a hand up.

"You've lost too much weight," she added. "If you're

going through something with your health, I'd like to know. I'd like to be there for you."

Her father's gaze went from her to Hudson and then to A.J.

"We can talk about it when we're not in mixed company," he said before walking out of the room.

It wasn't a denial. And now that the cat was out of the bag, he couldn't avoid the conversation much longer. She decided not to go after him.

Instead, she looked at Hudson. "How long are you staying?"

"My overnight bag is in my truck. Okay if I bunk here for the night?" he asked.

Maybe it was because she didn't know Hudson better than casual conversation but the thought of him sticking around didn't sit well. The thought of being under the same roof was worse.

"I'm headed out," she said to her half brother. "Make yourself comfortable in the guest room downstairs. I'll be back in the morning."

It had been a day and it was getting late. The idea of staying home held no appeal.

"Hey, take good care of my sister. She's practically a saint." Hudson nodded, gripped the neck of the bottle of beer and then headed down the hallway.

"Mind if I crash at your place tonight?" she asked A.J.

"Funny," he said, "I was just about to suggest the same thing."

THE DRIVE to the big house was quiet. A.J. had his own home out on the McGannon property, but he figured Tess would be more comfortable in the guest room she was familiar with. Plus, his place was almost an hour drive from the big house, in the wrong direction from where they were. It was taking them half an hour to get home as it was. He didn't want to add to the time.

Information swirled around in his head. A.J. didn't normally 'do' this much peopling in a day. Being around Tess was one thing. She didn't wear him out like the others did. He actually liked being with her and didn't want to admit just how happy it made him that she'd wanted to come home with him.

He could almost hear the gears grinding in her head on the way over and she needed a little time off from overthinking. At this point, all that would do was continue to stress her out more.

As he pulled into the gravel lot next to the big house, he asked, "Do you want to go for a walk or head straight inside?"

"Inside." She didn't hesitate and he realized being outside might bring back bad memories for her.

"Okay." He took care of Bear outside before walking her inside the house via the kitchen. "I'm pretty certain your dad will never forgive you for bringing a McGannon inside his house."

She broke into a smile at his comment.

"Yeah, that move is probably going to haunt me for a long time," she agreed.

"What do you think of Hudson?" He grabbed a couple of bottles of water on their way out of the kitchen.

"Now or in general?"

"Now." He was curious to get her perspective because his impression of the man wasn't good.

She shrugged as they walked down the hallway together, Bear trailing behind.

"I don't think about him all that much, actually. It's nice of him to come home to check on me. I think."

After following her into the bedroom, he set the bottled waters down. There was a basket of snacks that had been placed on the nightstand next to the bed. He'd thank Miss Penny for those later.

"Do you want to shower first?" He needed a shower and a fresh change of clothes.

"No, go ahead." She picked through the basket. "I'll stick around here and munch on a few snacks."

Bear hopped up on the bed and A.J. didn't have the heart to tell him to get down. He was a damn fine dog.

"I'll grab some clothes and come right back," he said. "You're good, right?"

"I can survive a few minutes without you, A.J., but I don't like much more than that if I'm honest. I haven't had a real friend in a very long time and I'm still a little scared." Those words hit home.

"Bear here will keep you company." All of A.J.'s protective instincts flared.

"I would've picked him anyway," she teased.

A.J. ran to his old bedroom. He kept plenty of clothes there. Sometimes it was just easier to crash at the big house, depending on where he was working on the ranch that day. His freedom was something he'd always prized.

It was one of the many reasons he'd convinced himself that he didn't want to be with someone who tied him down. He liked to come and go as he pleased, without answering to anyone but himself.

So, why did that sound so lonely now?

He'd been a loner without being lonely for most of his life. Tess was changing that, changing him.

Rather than run blindly down that trail, he refocused on getting something to wear. He pulled an outfit from his closet, and fresh undergarments from the dresser. He also found a couple of old T-shirts that were two sizes too big on him and would swallow Tess, but she might be more comfortable sleeping in one of those than in the clothes she'd been wearing for most of the day.

There were plenty of supplies in the guest bath, so he didn't concern himself with bringing a toothbrush or toothpaste. After loading up with clothes, he jogged back down to the guest room where Tess waited on the bed.

She'd brought the basket over and was picking through it again when he returned.

"I have clothes." He set the folded bundle down next to Bear.

The whole no-sleeping-on-the-bed rule had been blown to bits the first night Bear had come home. He'd been scared but it was cold outside and, apparently, the heat from A.J.'s blanket was too tempting to pass up. By morning, Bear was curled up against A.J.'s leg.

"Sorry if that's not allowed." She motioned toward Bear.

"This guy gets to do pretty much anything he wants," A.J. said.

"He's sweet and I'm not just saying that because he saved my life." She reached over to pet him.

The dog practically mewled like a kitty.

"Tough guy there." A.J. laughed on his way to the bathroom.

"Hey." Tess's voice stopped him.

He turned around.

"I used to think you were pretty arrogant. You know. Like you had an answer for everything, and you knew all there was to know…"

"Thank you?" He chuckled. "If you are trying to give me a compliment, you should know that you're really bad at it."

"No, silly. I just mean there is so much to you that's unexpected. That's all."

"I'm going to take that as a positive." He arched a brow and puffed his chest out.

That made her laugh. Man, it was good to hear that sound. Her laugh had a musical quality to it that hit him square in the chest, made him want to hear more. It was a shame the dire circumstances that had brought them together. He wanted more of that lighter sound that made him think everything in the world could right itself.

Rather than get inside his head over that commentary, he excused himself and took a shower. Brushing his teeth and washing up was heaven. He skipped the shave figuring he could get away with another day or two without one.

When he stepped out of the bathroom, Tess tilted her head to one side and asked, "Why did you think it was a good idea for me to come here tonight?"

T ess was curious as to why he thought his
ranch would be safe for her.

A.J. moved to the side of the bed and
took a knee. "Do you want to take a shower next?"

"You didn't answer my question. Why were you
about to ask me the same question back at my ranch?"
She wasn't letting him get off the hook that easily. If
there was something about her home that bothered
him, she needed to know.

"For one, I noticed your house doesn't have an
alarm system and there's no security on the property to
speak of," he started.

Fair enough.

"For another thing, you seemed on edge there.
Here, you're more relaxed. Plus, I thought you could
use a good night of sleep and, not to brag, but you did
okay sleeping in my arms last night."

Now, she regretted bringing it up. A.J. was observant. She'd give him that. She didn't want to admit or acknowledge just how well she'd slept. The Tess of a few days ago would have balked at the idea of merely wanting to be in the same room with A.J. McGannon. Now, he seemed like her lifeline.

"It's true. Being in my house again gave me the creeps. I'm sure it's just because of what happened and the tension with my father. Once I get past the fact that I was attacked on our land, I'll be strong enough to tackle the place on my own."

"Have you thought about having an alarm system installed? It might go a long way toward giving you peace of mind," he said. "Especially if your father is going to be away for weeks on end."

"I could always come here." Her comment was off-hand, and there was a split second of panic as she realized that she'd spoken without thinking.

"You'd be welcome any time." The speed of his response sent goose bumps up and down her arms.

"I appreciate it. I do. But I have to get my bearings again at some point. Put this whole...*mess*...behind me."

"You will." The fact there was no hesitation in his voice almost made her believe it, too.

"I'm not looking forward to telling my father that I don't want to work the ranch anymore."

"I didn't realize you were considering leaving

Clemente Cattle." Eyes wide, mouth open, he seemed startled by her statement.

It was good to try it out on someone besides her father because he was going to have a conniption. He'd been grooming her to take over the family business from birth.

"The thought of hurting my father has held me back from making any announcements. I can't even find the right words to tell him." She stopped when A.J. shot her a look. "What?"

"You haven't been scared of challenging me at every turn," he said.

"Who said I was afraid of telling my father?"

A.J. didn't respond verbally. His expression said it all. Mouth clamped shut. Eyes focused off to the side of the room. And a *seriously?* look stamped on his face.

"It's not the same thing. There's no comparison," she argued.

He locked gazes with her. "Okay. Tell me how, but I'm not convinced at the moment."

"For one, I love my father too much to hurt him."

"Let me ask this. How do know if it'll hurt him if you don't explain how you feel?"

Oh, damn.

"Okay, good point," she conceded.

"I'm not a parent but my guess is the main hope is that your children end up happy," he said.

"Right. But my father has expectations. You've met him, right?"

He nodded.

"You just saw him in action. He shuts me out and still tries to tell me what to do." Her arguments were weak now that she heard them said out loud. She held her hand up to stop A.J. from calling her on it. "Which doesn't mean he couldn't get over the fact that I don't want to work the ranch."

"What do you want to do?"

"Social work. But when I told my dad that I wanted to go to UT instead of A&M to get a social work degree he flipped." The conversation hadn't gone well, and she still remembered how hurt he'd seemed.

"What's your degree in?"

"Social work." She leveled her gaze at him and smiled.

"How did you manage that if he was against it?"

"I'm afraid that I'm not following," she said.

"How is that your father wanted you to go to one school and yet you convinced him to let you go to the one you wanted *and* get the degree you liked best?" He picked through the contents of the basket, looking for a snack.

"I explained to him that my heart was in social work. I told him how important it was to me. But he made me promise that I'd come home to work the ranch. He said I could get a degree in anything that I wanted because he'd basically taught me everything I needed to know to run the ranch by then anyway," she explained.

"So, you stood your ground and he compromised."
A.J. selected a bag of cheese-flavored crackers and then
took a seat. "Sounds like you know how to get what
you really want when you put your mind to it."

The argument of not wanting to hurt her father
was losing steam. She'd pushed to get her degree in the
field she'd wanted and then conceded her life. "Okay,
McGannon, I see what you're doing here. It all sounds
so easy when you put it like that."

"I never said it was easy." He popped one of the
cheese crackers in his mouth and took his time chew-
ing. "I just said you know how to stick to your guns
when you really want something."

She couldn't argue his point, no matter how much
she wanted to. In life, she'd taken the easy way out
because she didn't want to keep battling with a father
she loved who only wanted good things for her.

Maybe she could suggest a compromise. Her half-
brother seemed to run a successful business. She
wondered if she could talk to her father about bringing
Hudson into the family trade.

"Say it," A.J.'s voice was a tease.

"What?"

"That I'm right." His slight smirk was infuriating.
Rather than give into his taunting, she stood up and
said, "I'd rather take a shower."

"Together?" he quipped.

"Not a chance, McGannon." There should be more
conviction in those words than she could muster.

"Shame," he said so quietly she almost couldn't hear him.

A.J. shouldn't tease Tess. Granted, she needed a distraction. But their friendship was just gaining its footing.

If someone had asked him if he would care this much about her feelings last week, his response would've been laughter. Life had a way of turning upside down when he least expected it. There were times when that flip hurt like hell, as in the case of his father. And there were times when it brought the most unexpected light into his life.

Being with Tess was also a game-changer for future friendships. She was intelligent and funny. Her strength blew him away. Her compassion for others was another strong suit—one he hadn't seen coming given their history. Of course, he'd been busy trying to push her buttons before. Rattling her cage had become sport.

She gave as good as she got. A.J. was pretty certain Tess liked picking fights with him. They'd become sparring partners of sorts.

So, he didn't expect to like her this much as he got to know her better. He'd always respected her. Her quick wit and intelligence had caused him to lose as many arguments as he'd won. Could she be frustrat-ingly stubborn?

The answer to that question was a hard yes. Seeing the softer side to her, the compassionate side, broke down many of his carefully constructed walls. He liked being around her more than he cared to admit.

A part of him picked that time to argue he *needed* to be around her, but he blocked that noise out pretty quick. He couldn't afford to think that way. Tess Clemente had the power to rock his world. There was no way he planned to hand that over without a fight.

He was already at a disadvantage now that he liked her. Getting into a fight over the location of a tree and a building seemed pretty damn silly to him now.

Part of him could admit that it had been fun to fight with her on some level. He'd liked the way she'd challenged him and made him see a situation in a new light. She'd kept his mind sharp.

And he was competitive enough to hate losing.

The water cut off in the next room and he finished up the snack he'd been holding but forgot to eat while he was preoccupied thinking about her.

"I probably should be tired," she admitted as she walked out of the bathroom. His heart stirred and his pulse kicked up a few notches when he looked at her.

He didn't want to notice how right it felt to see her in his family home wearing his oversized T-shirt and boxers. But he did. He couldn't help himself.

He also didn't want to be transfixed by a bead of

water as it rolled down the delicate lines of her neck. But he was. Her wet hair was slicked back away from her face and he could see her beautiful long lines more clearly.

And he sure as hell didn't want to follow that water droplet as it rolled down her neck and onto her full breasts. But he did that, too.

Way to go, McGannon. He was doing a real great job of keeping his feelings in check.

"You've had the kind of day that can keep the mind spinning," he said.

"I keep thinking about Rhett and feeling sorry for him. Don't get me wrong, if I thought he was guilty, I'd be mad as hell. He has worked so hard to control his impulses and get in a better place. He's had so much success. I should probably toughen up and face facts."

"It's human to want the best for others. It shows how much you care about your clients and the work that you do." He wanted her to know just how much he admired her for everything she was doing.

"It's not good to be naïve, though. I could be putting others in danger."

"When I first started working with Bear, I took his setbacks personally. There were times when he just couldn't get inside the truck, no matter many times I reassured him. I eventually learned that he had a different timetable and he needed to come into his own. All I could do was provide the right encouragement. I could show him that he could trust me, but after being burned that might take time."

She was rocking her head and he hoped that his message was really getting through.

"All we can do is offer the right support and encouragement. It's not up to us if it's taken or ignored," he added.

After sitting in silence for a few minutes, contemplating, she scooched over to Bear. "How'd your owner get so smart?"

Bear rolled onto his back in the ultimate show of trust for a dog. He'd always been a sucker for a good belly rub.

Tess laughed and the sound was like bubbles floating on a breeze. And before he could wax poetic, he fished his phone out and checked the screen.

His heart nearly stopped when he saw the messages from his brothers.

Tess must've been watching his expression because she immediately asked, "What is it? What's going on?"

"Dad is waking up."

14

Tess had never seen A.J. move so fast out of a chair. He was so quick to get dressed that he didn't leave the room and her pulse skyrocketed as she did her level best to look away from toned abs.

"Is it weird that I want to come with you?" she asked, and it wasn't because she was scared to be at his house by herself. "I genuinely want to see how your father is doing and I'd like to be there for you for a change if that's okay. It would give me the chance to start repaying some of the kindness you've shown me."

A.J. smiled and it was devastating to her heart. "I'll set out food for Bear in case we're not back by morning. He'll be fine inside the house while we're gone. There's almost always someone here."

That might change with the news his father was

waking up. Everyone would want to be by Mr. McGannon's side when he opened his eyes for the first time.

Tess was on her feet, darting into the bathroom to change in a half second. By the time she finished putting on the fresh jogging suit that had been laid out for her, A.J. stood at the door to the hallway. Keys in one hand, cell in the other, he tapped his finger on the doorjamb as he waited for her.

She gave Bear a quick hug and promised to be back soon.

A.J. was quiet, serious, on the way to the hospital. Knowing him like she did now, he probably didn't want to get his hopes up and she couldn't blame him. Hope was the only emotion that could be more dangerous than fear.

He parked the truck in a row of similar-looking ones, all with *McGannon Herd* logos on the right-hand side of the back window. A.J. was out of the pickup and on her side faster than she could unbuckle her seatbelt.

She'd gotten so close to A.J. in the past couple of days that she'd almost forgot the fact that their families were almost constantly at odds. She looked him in the eyes and asked, "Do you think it'll be okay with everyone that I'm here with you?"

"I wouldn't have brought you if I didn't." There was so much sincerity in his hazel-brown eyes that she believed him.

A few minutes later, walking into the special

hospital suite filled with his family, she realized he was right. There were definitely more than a few stares and a couple of jaws nearly hit the floor. But if there was one person in the room who didn't like her, she couldn't pick them out.

Instead, one-by-one, she was greeted by his brothers first, Levi, Ryan, Dalton, Jack, and Declan. And then by cousins Reed, Hayden, Coby, Brant, and Cage.

Growing up an only child and a girl, she was struck by how much testosterone could be in one room. And there was no denying that any McGannon could easily be on a billboard in Times Square selling underwear or men's clothing.

There were two couples in the room; Levi and Ensley, and Ryan and Alexis. Ensley's family had moved away following the tragic death of her younger brother years ago. Alexis Haley, now McGannon, had grown up in Cattle Cove before moving to Houston after high school graduation.

Both women greeted Tess with a warm hug.

Miss Penny was there with Hawk, and Donny stood near the door. Tess couldn't tell if he was trying to greet people or ready to make a quick exit.

"The doctor is in with Dad," Levi said to A.J. "Dalton was in when it happened. He can tell you better in his own words."

Dalton was sitting on the bench with his hands clasped and his elbows resting on his knees. "I was sitting by his bed with my hand resting on his arm. I could've sworn I felt movement. After that, I must've stared at his hand for five minutes straight. And then I saw his finger twitch. The buzzer was right there, and I didn't want to leave his side so I buzzed in the nurse."

"That's a good sign, right?" The hope in A.J.'s voice nearly melted her.

"The doctor said it could be," Dalton supplied. "He's in there now and they're hooking Dad up to a couple more machines."

"How long has he been in there?" A.J. asked.

"He's been in and out." Dalton picked up a cup of coffee that was sitting on the table beside him. "First sign of progress in a long time."

"I guess now we wait." A.J.'s sentiment was met with a few nods.

Donny excused himself before disappearing down the hallway. Tess had never really gotten a good feel for the man and he seemed especially nervous now.

A knock at the opened door caused all eyes to fly to the person standing there.

"Can we help you?" Levi asked; he'd always seemed to be the one to take the lead and, being the oldest, his brothers had always shown him a little extra respect.

A man stood there who looked to be close in age to Levi, and the weird thing was that he looked exactly like the other McGannons.

"My name is Kurt Johnson." He looked around the room, taking in all the faces with a little bit of surprise and maybe a little disdain. "I understand this is Clive McGannon's room."

It was so quiet Tess could hear a pin drop.

And then Levi spoke up. "Can I ask what your business is here with my father?"

Kurt made a show of throwing his arms out in mock welcome. "Is that any kind of question for your brother?"

A.J. STOOD up and put himself in between his brother and Kurt before Levi did something he'd regret, like punch the man. A.J. didn't want his brother thrown out and this crackpot must have been drinking or something to show up and make a claim like that.

"Can I ask where you've been?" Levi's hands fisted at his sides and his jaw clenched.

"What? No McGannon family welcome to their long-lost brother?" Kurt teased. The man was walking on thin ice. Walking? Hell, he was stomping up and down where he shouldn't be.

"Our father isn't feeling well—"

"Oh, really? I received a phone call that said he was waking up." Every one of Kurt's words were issued like a challenge.

And it wasn't exactly sitting well with anyone in the room based on the tension that had just ratcheted up.

"Let's go have a talk, just you and me." A.J. physically moved the guy into the hallway. If this had been a bar, there would have been a fight. But A.J. respected his father too much to throw fists at this point and this guy was probably delusional anyway.

A.J. couldn't argue with the fact that the man looked like one of them. And he figured this was an Uncle Donny problem. Which basically meant they'd all pay the price for his indiscretion.

Once he got Kurt out into the hallway, he asked, "I don't know who you are or why you decided to show up now. But I do have one question. Are you trying to get your butt kicked?"

Kurt puffed up. He was tall enough to look A.J. and his brothers dead in the eye, and the guy worked out. There was no denying that.

"What's your problem?" Kurt shot back.

"You. Showing up in my dad's hospital room, making trouble."

Kurt threw his hands in the surrender position and took a couple of steps back. "Hey, man, I didn't come here to start trouble. I just reacted to it when it stared me in the face."

"Which still doesn't explain what you're doing here."

"Donny warned me you guys would freak out once you saw me," he said.

"Only because you showed up making an ass of yourself. I don't know what kind of game you're playing—"

Kurt stopped A.J. cold with one look. He paused long enough to let it sink in. Then, he shook his head. "That's just it. I don't play games. I came to check on the father I just found out that I had."

"Wait. You didn't know who your father was?" A.J. could hear the shock in his own tone.

"Why does that surprise you?"

"Uncle Donny is usually the one who..." A.J. left the sentence dangling. He didn't have the right words to finish it anyway.

"Well, he's not my father. Clive McGannon is. I came to meet him."

"There's a little problem with that right now." A.J. was not sure if he should pity the guy or be angry. The man could have a mental issue.

"Oh, yeah? What's that?" Kurt asked.

"He's been in a coma for weeks. The first encouraging sign he might come out on the other side happened a little while ago. But it wasn't much, and the doc has been in with him for a while. The way you came into Dad's hospital suite like a bull in a china shop isn't helping your case, especially if you want to be part of this family at some point." A.J. sized Kurt up. Physically, he could easily pass for a McGannon. But then again, he could be A.J.'s cousin as easily as he could be his brother.

Either way, he wasn't exactly winning any popularity contests with any of the family.

"Look, I came in expecting a fight and that's what I

gave you guys. You have every reason to hate me now. Guess what? I'm not here to be your friend. I'm here to get to the bottom of why I'm just now finding out that man in there is my father."

"You're telling me that you had no idea?" Now, A.J. really was shocked.

"Not until Donny McGannon located me out of the blue and told me that my father was in the hospital. He was the one who said I should come and he told me to buck up for a fight." Kurt folded his arms over his chest. "So, I'm here."

"Fighting is optional. It sounds like all we need is a DNA test to clear this up." A.J. put this down to a mix-up. If anything, this guy was Donny's son. There was no way he belonged to A.J.'s dad. "How old are you anyway?"

"I'm thirty-five years old. Why?"

"My dad was married and expecting his first child with my mother when you were born." If A.J. was having this conversation about Uncle Donny, it would be a no-brainer. But A.J.'s parents had loved each other deeply. Given Kurt's age, he had to belong to Donny if he was a McGannon at all.

A thought nagged A.J. about his logic. Why would Uncle Donny be the one to bring Kurt to the hospital if he was lying?

Tess peeked out of the suite. "Everything okay out here?"

She was a sight for sore eyes.

"Yeah. We were just trying to figure out what Uncle Donny is up to," A.J. said. He turned to Kurt. "My dad is here and so are you. We're in a hospital. I can't think of a better place for a DNA test."

"So be it."

"Follow me." A.J. started toward the suite.

"Hold on a second. I'm not going back in there with that wolf pack."

A.J. had heard his family called a lot of names over the years but this was a new one. He couldn't hold in the chuckle at the reference. "Here's the deal. You didn't get off on the right foot a few minutes ago with my brothers and cousins. But if it turns out that you're one of us, you won't find a better *pack* to have your back in life. If you mess with one of us, you mess with all of us."

That seemed to resonate with Kurt as he nodded.

"If you lie to us, there's no greater enemy," A.J. warned.

Kurt threw his hands up again. "I already told you that someone called me, not the other way around. I didn't come here looking for a problem. I'd like to know who my father is. That's all. I don't want anything from your family."

"Then we both want the same things." A.J. led Kurt back into the room where everyone was standing around the doctor. The door to his father's suite was open. He put a hand up to Kurt, who acknowledged this wasn't the time to bring up his parenting issue.

A.J. stood just inside the door. Tess linked their fingers and a calmness he hadn't felt washed over him.

"There could still be a long road ahead of us," the doctor explained. "This is a positive sign that he could be waking up. With traumatic brain injury patients, we can never be certain what that will look like. This is very much an individual case-by-case situation but it is encouraging that he still has brain function. I'm sorry I can't give you a more definitive answer."

"You said this is basically a miracle," Ensley said.

"Yes. So, it's a good thing I believe in them. I've seen a lot over the years, Mrs. McGannon. Most of it can be explained by medicine, science. Then there are those cases that leave you scratching your head and believing that maybe someone else has been in charge all along." Dr. Gregory had been caring for Cattle Cove and the surrounding areas more than twenty-five years. "I'll keep you up to date should his condition change. Right now, we can be happy about your father's progress."

"Thank you, Doctor." Levi extended a hand. The doctor shook it before acknowledging the rest of the room with a nod.

A.J. leaned toward his cousin, Reed, who stood next to him and said, "Can you get a hold of your father? We need him here."

Reed was the oldest cousin and was six months younger than Levi. The two had been in the same grade and were close. Reed also had the most disdain for his old man. He'd been old enough to know what was happening despite the best efforts to protect them.

"Is he the reason for that guy?" Reed nodded toward Kurt.

"Afraid so," A.J. responded.

The doctor started to leave but A.J. stopped him before he could pass. "Any chance you have a DNA kit somewhere around? We have a paternity question."

Miss Penny had been watching the events unfold, keeping a curious eye on Kurt. Hawk seemed downright ready to take the stranger outside and teach him some manners, but he was just being protective.

"I can have a nurse help you with that," Dr. Gregory said. "I'll send someone right in."

15

A fter the consent forms had been signed, Levi had power of attorney over his father while he was in a coma so that made things easier, they were told that the results wouldn't take longer than the average lunch.

With his dad's condition the same as it had been, which was no improvement, A.J. was only sticking around the hospital to find out if Kurt was crazy and see if his brothers needed him to do anything about it.

Uncle Donny had disappeared and wasn't answering Reed's texts, or anyone else's for that matter.

"This might sound like a jerk question, but how do you grow up not knowing who your father is?" Reed wasn't trying to be offensive.

"I grew up with the last name Johnson. My mother told me she got pregnant during a one-time fling with an older man while she was in college. By the time she figured out she was pregnant he was long gone." Kurt shrugged. "I didn't have a reason to doubt her."

"Do you mind if I ask your mother's first name?" Miss Penny took the lead next.

"Katherine."

Miss Penny shook her head and the guys knew she was saying that she'd never heard of her. Then again, if their father had had an affair during his marriage, he wouldn't exactly be proud of the fact. If the two didn't speak to each other or their father didn't know about the child, there'd be nothing to discuss.

"You never asked about who your father was?" Miss Penny knew how to ask delicate questions without coming off unsympathetic.

"I didn't think about it that much. If I did, I would've been too young to remember anyway." He shrugged. "Plus, what good would it do? I mean, I figured what was the use?"

"And now you've conveniently changed your tune?" Levi said before apologizing. The situation was tense.

"Not conveniently. Donny McGannon contacted me and said my father was in the hospital and that I deserved to meet him before it was too late."

No wonder Donny had disappeared. He'd stirred up the pot and now he was hiding during the fallout. Typical Donny. Some things would never change, and it was one of the many reasons A.J. didn't trust the man.

"I didn't come right away. I thought that it didn't

matter to me who my father was. It wasn't like he was around when my mom got sick and I had to help make decisions for her when I was barely eighteen. What did it matter now?" Kurt's voice held so much reverence when he talked about his mother.

Damn. A.J. didn't want to pity the guy. He'd wanted to deck him. Until now.

"Except that every time I look into my little girl's face, I wonder if she looks like my dad. I wonder if she laughs like him. Or has any of his traits. Except I don't know what those are. So, after sitting on the information for weeks, I decided to come and see for myself."

A nurse knocked on the door. She held a piece of paper in her hand.

There was a collective gasp before the entire room went dead quiet. A.J. could hear a pin drop.

"I have the paternity results here." The nurse held the paper in two hands like she was holding dynamite and didn't want to drop it. She looked at Kurt. "Clive McGannon is a close enough match to your DNA to assume he's your father and not your uncle."

It took a minute for everyone to absorb the shock of that news, including Kurt.

"I hope this is good news," the nurse said before excusing herself.

"I really thought the guy who called me had lost his mind after I looked up who Clive McGannon is," Kurt said, obviously still stunned.

Levi stood up and everyone sort of held their breath for what felt like a long moment. He made a beeline for Kurt who bucked up, expecting a fight, before extending his hand. His half-brother relaxed into the handshake.

"Welcome to the family, brother," Levi said, and the others followed suit.

A stunned Kurt shook each hand as one-by-one introductions were made.

"You said you had a daughter?" Levi again took the lead.

"Yeah. Paisley. She'll be a year old next month," Kurt supplied.

"We'd like to meet her," Levi said on behalf of the family.

Kurt looked at him wearily.

"I mean it. No hard feelings. You're family. It's probably best if we start over and get to know each other a little bit," Levi continued.

"I'm new to this whole big family thing. I grew up an only child and this is all a little much to take. How many of you are there?" Kurt turned the tables.

"In total? There are six of us who are Clive's sons and five who are Donny's. You probably figured out that Clive and Donny are brothers."

Kurt nodded.

"I hate to interrupt, but since there's no change with Dad, I'm going to head home with Tess." A.J. figured this whole scenario would be playing out for a long time. It was getting late and Tess needed rest. "She's crashing in the guest room for now."

Heads nodded in unison. Both Ensley and Alexis smiled, and it reminded him that they, too, had spent time in that same room recently. He wanted to tell them that this wasn't the same thing but figured it was best to leave that topic alone.

Tess held onto his hand and, as expected, they got a few looks for it. No doubt, questions swirled in a few of his family members' minds. He could explain everything later. Now, he needed to get her home and to bed.

A.J. liked the sound of those last words a little too much than was good for him. He looked to Kurt. "It was nice to meet you. I'm sure we'll catch up later."

"Thanks for straightening me out earlier," Kurt walked over and shook A.J.'s hand.

"No problem. We'll be in touch."

A.J. reclaimed Tess's hand and linked their fingers. He walked her to the truck all the while his brain trying to wrap around the fact his father had had an affair. There was an entirely new family member. Life could turn upside down on a dime, no warning, no chance to absorb news.

He stopped at the passenger side.

"It's been a crazy few days and...well...I know we said this is a bad idea and it probably is, but, damn, I'd like your permission to kiss you again."

Tess practically beamed up at him and his heart took another hit.

"Permission granted, McGannon."

That was all the encouragement he needed to claim those pink lips of hers. There was so much passion and heat in the kiss he could only imagine what might happen if they let this go further.

What would it be like if they took their hands off the reins for a minute and let this thing between them take off? The sex would be amazing. No, better than that. It would be mind-blowing in the best possible way.

There was so much heat and promise in that one kiss that when their lips parted, it took a second for him to catch his breath. His heart drummed against his rib cage and his pulse skyrocketed.

"Damn," he said low and under his breath.

"I was just about to say the same thing." Tess's voice was barely above a whisper. Still, it was the sexiest sound he'd heard all day.

"Are you sure we're making a mistake when we kiss? Because I'd be happy to move forward with this thing happening between us. I'm pretty certain sex with you would be the best thing I've ever experienced," he said, knowing it would be so much more than that.

"Yeah?" she teased.

"Yes."

She tugged at his shirt until their bodies were flush

and her back was against the truck. Her tongue darted across her bottom lip, leaving a silky trail.

"Sex with you would be pretty amazing, McGannon. I don't doubt that one bit." She feathered a kiss against his lips.

He couldn't help it. He smiled.

"But then what?" she asked. "What would be next? Because it would change everything for me and I'm not sure I could ever go back to the way it was before."

"Are you saying you could now?" Being with her had changed him in ways he still hadn't processed. Amid all the chaos going on in his life he needed a minute to figure out what that meant.

"I could try. Maybe in the future. Right now, I need to clear the air with my father."

Before he could respond to the bomb she dropped, she climbed inside the cab and fastened her seatbelt.

THE DRIVE to her family's ranch was spent in silence. They'd picked up Bear on the way. As A.J. parked, she asked, "Does that gym bag in the back have fresh clothes in it?"

He nodded.

"Why don't you bring it in and get comfortable. Take a shower. Wait for me in my room," she exited the vehicle with Bear on her heels.

"Okay." A.J. grabbed the bag and followed her inside.

She deposited them both in her bedroom and showed him the en suite bathroom. Once A.J. and Bear were settled, she searched the house for her father and found him in his office.

"Dad, I love you and I'm sorry if what I'm about to tell you isn't the plan you had in mind for me. This is my life and I feel strongly about how I want to spend my future. And you need to know where I stand."

Her father sat behind his desk, arms folded across his chest. He'd always been a stoic man, but he looked tired to her. "And where is that, Tess?"

Standing up for what she wanted after her father had carefully constructed her future out of care wasn't going to be easy. Of course, she hadn't expected it to be a cakewalk. The thought of disappointing one of the people she cared most about in the world was a thousand-pound gorilla on her back. "I got a degree in social work for a reason. It's what I care about more than anything else. It's where I feel the most needed—"

"You don't feel needed here?"

"Maybe *needed* isn't the right word." This was more difficult to put into words than she'd expected. Maybe he could relate if she turned the tables. It was worth a shot. "What about you? What's the one thing you've always wanted to do in life?"

"That's easy. Own this ranch. Create a legacy for my

child." The fact that he'd had no hesitation reminded her just how passionate he was about the life he'd built. And she hoped she could capitalize on that to help him understand where her passion resided.

"What would you say if someone had told you early on that cattle ranching was a bad idea? What if someone told you that you had to own a restaurant—"

He was already shaking his head. "I can't cook and, besides, I've always known what I wanted to do."

There was no questioning where her stubborn streak had come from and it caused her to smile.

"This ranch is your passion project, and you've built an amazing business. *You* have. Not me. As much as I love the land, this isn't my dream. It's yours."

She let those words sit for a minute between them.

Shock didn't begin to describe her when he didn't immediately react. Instead, he seemed to be contemplating her point of view. After a few minutes passed, he stood up and motioned toward the twin leather chairs that were nestled around a coffee table. She'd spent more years than she cared to count in one of those chairs being taught how to run the family business. She'd learned just how much ranching was about paperwork and getting the details right.

She took the seat across from her father, preparing for one of his counterarguments. In this light, she could see how much he'd aged and how much weaker he looked from his medical treatments—treatments that they'd recently learned weren't working.

"What about my legacy to you, Tess?" Gone was any sign of judgment from his features.

"Your legacy to me doesn't have anything to do with these walls or the land. What you've given me is so much more than that. You've shown me how to work hard for what I want. By your example, I know to dig my heels in when something is really important to me. I've learned there's always more ways than one to solve a problem. You've handed down a love of all animals, big and small."

He clasped his hands together and rested his elbows on his thighs. If she didn't know better, she'd say her father's eyes were watering.

"You've taught me to be honest and fair. And you've given me unconditional love. I can't think of better gifts than those. That's your legacy to me."

A rogue tear slid down her father's face.

He coughed a couple of times before he spoke. "No one will ever accuse me of being a perfect father. A lot of times I worried my mistakes would hurt you so much that you wouldn't recover."

"Mistakes are powerful teachers, Dad. There's nothing wrong with making a mistake. The best gift you've ever given me is your love."

He leaned back and looked out the window for a long moment. "What will you do with the ranch when I'm gone?"

"I'd like to ask your permission to sell to someone who will love the property as much as we have," she said. The thought of leaving was hard, but she couldn't imagine running this place and continuing the work she loved.

He nodded. "Do you have a person in mind?"

"Not off the top of my head but I have no doubt we'll find someone," she said. "It might come as a shock to you, but I love this land. I have no interest in running the business, but this place will always be part of my heart."

"The McGannons would buy it in a heartbeat," he offered.

"Would that make you happy knowing who would be taking over the reins?" She searched his face for signs of disappointment in her. She was pretty certain that she saw relief instead.

"It would," he said. "They know what they're doing, and they'll take good care of the herd."

"Then, we'll talk to them whenever you're rea—"

"We have a deal on the table already," he said, cutting her off.

"Why didn't you say something before?"

"I wasn't planning to go through with the offer. They'll let me live out the rest of my life here before taking over if that's agreeable to you. The money will set you up for a long time."

Given the property's worth, she wouldn't have to work a day in her life if she didn't want to. But she did want to. This would free her up to take the job of her heart instead of one that put a roof over her head. And she could do a lot of good with the excess funds by donating to charitable causes that were close to her heart. She'd always wanted to run a sanctuary. The ranch would be perfect, but the land was more valuable than the cattle, so she'd have to compromise.

She could, however, purchase a small piece of land that could house rescue animals.

"You've given me so many gifts in my life, Dad. I hope I haven't disappointed you too much." She meant those words with her whole heart.

"Oh, darlin'. You could never be a disappointment to me. I'm sorry if I gave you that impression. I love the ranch but not more than I love you."

Those words stirred up so many emotions inside Tess; love, joy, happiness. Relief.

"I love you, Dad."

"I haven't said those words nearly enough to you, Tess. I love you, too."

No one was ever guaranteed a tomorrow. Tess was grateful for the time she had left with her father. It might not be more than a few months, half a year if they were lucky, but she planned to make every day count.

"Then, I think we should take the McGannons up on their offer, Dad."

Her father smiled. She couldn't honestly remember seeing him do that nearly enough in her lifetime.

"Dad, we're going to be okay. You know that, right?" She hadn't discussed his illness or what that might mean to both of their lives. They'd covered a lot of ground in one conversation and she'd leave it at that. For now.

He stood up, walked over, and did something he'd only done a couple of times in her entire life...wrapped her in a hug.

16

T ess walked out of her father's office and back to the bedroom where she found A.J. and Bear. She moved to the bed near Bear and sat down.

"I just got a text. Rhett Daniels has been arrested," A.J. informed her. He still had on the same clothes and she figured he must've been distracted by the text.

The news, although not unexpected, still stunned her.

"Where did they find him?" she asked. "I'm still not convinced he's responsible."

"McKinney State Falls," he said. "He was camping, just like he said."

"This is so not good for him, is it?"

"Maybe this will give him a chance to clear himself." A.J.'s words offered a little hope into an otherwise dark situation. She hoped it was true.

"How'd it go with your father?" A.J. asked, redirecting the conversation.

"Great, actually. He took it really well." She'd tell him all about the sale later. Right now, she wanted a snack, a shower, and a bed. Tess bit back a yawn. "I'm heading to the kitchen. Do you want something?"

"I'll meet you there. I'm just going to take that shower real quick," A.J. said.

"Mind if Bear comes with me?"

"Not at all." A.J. hopped up and moved to the adjacent bathroom.

Bear walked into the kitchen and straight to the back door.

"Do you need to go outside?" She scratched him in his favorite spot right behind the ears.

He answered by wagging his tail even harder.

She opened the door and walked outside.

"Hey, Tess, I found your phone." Hudson held up a cell from across the lawn. He was visible from the light over the barn door.

"What are you doing out here?" It was getting late and being near the barn caused a shiver to race down her back. It made sense, though. This is where she'd been when she'd lost her phone.

"Come on, Bear." She could kill two birds with one stone this way. She covered the distance between the house and barn in a jog.

Facing this exact spot again was something she was going to have to do at some point. At least she had Bear by her side and that kept her from freaking out.

Hudson reached into his pocket and palmed something small. He put his hand out to Bear. "Here's a treat, big guy."

"He shouldn't eat extra food because—"

Her words fell on deaf ears. Hudson fed the morsel to Bear anyway.

"It's time he and I made friends," Hudson said by way of explanation.

For reasons she couldn't pinpoint, she didn't like the idea. She also felt uneasy being here but that was most likely because this was the exact spot she was attacked. Bad memories surfaced of where she woke.

Bear started yacking and she dropped down beside him.

"Bear...are you okay?"

A white foam filled his mouth and he seemed to be struggling to breathe. Her mind immediately snapped to an allergic reaction.

"What did you give him?" she asked Hudson. In that moment, it occurred to her investigators had scoured this area for her cell. They hadn't found it because it wasn't there. Hudson had had it all along. He'd been smart enough not to use it and he probably disabled any tracking software. Her half-brother was behind the attack.

Rhett was in jail and he seemed like the only suspect so far.

As she looked up, she caught a glimpse of a rock coming down toward her head. She put her hand up to block a second too late.

A.J. FINISHED his shower and walked into the bedroom. Tess was nowhere to be found. Bear had been her near-constant companion and A.J. assumed he'd find the two together. He threw on a pair of jeans and a shirt before heading into the kitchen.

It was getting late and his stomach reminded him he'd had a light dinner. That's probably where she was anyway.

He walked past her father's office on the way to the kitchen. The door was closed, and he didn't hear voices, so he didn't bother Mr. Clemente. The man would get used to A.J.'s presence eventually. Or, at least, that was the hope. He would see that A.J. cared about his daughter.

Again, it might just be a hope, but A.J. would like Tess's father to at the very least accept their friendship. A.J. hoped to be part of Tess's life moving forward. He didn't have a handle on what that meant just yet. All he knew for certain was that she'd become very special to him.

There was another guest in the home that A.J. couldn't get a good feel for. Hudson Leonard. Was it possible Tess was with her half-brother?

A.J. circled back toward the bedrooms. Hudson's door was open. The light was off. He was nowhere to be found.

Back in the kitchen, A.J. poured a glass of water, he looked out the back window, hoping to find Tess and Bear. In the dim light over the barn door in the distance, he saw what looked like a lump on the ground. That lump was familiar.

A.J. dropped the glass, it shattered in the sink, but he didn't care. He got the hell out of there and bolted toward Bear. Heart in his throat, he dropped down to his best friend's side as desperation slammed into him.

Bear's eyes rolled back in his head and he was convulsing.

Jesus, no. A.J. wasn't a praying man but he broke that rule right then and there, praying that Bear would come out of this. There was no way he could lose his best friend. A boulder docked on his chest, making it difficult to take in air. *Bear.* "Come on, buddy. You're gonna be okay."

He did his best to soothe the sweet animal as he blinked back tears. There was someone else missing in this equation.

"Tess," he shouted when she was nowhere to be found. Fear ripped through him when he didn't get a response. If she was around, she would've heard him. Panic seized his lungs, making breathing hurt. Adrenaline spiked, causing his pulse to race. He fisted his hands so tight there was no blood left by the time he flexed his fingers again. Anger roared through him. He'd never felt so helpless in all his life.

He *had* to find her alive. Period. There was no other outcome. He wouldn't allow himself to consider any other possibility.

A.J.'s gaze went straight to the ground where he tried to pick up a trail. It looked like someone had been dragged away from the barn.

A jolt of fear rocketed through him as he fished his cell out of his pocket. He immediately phoned the family vet, Derick Jacobs, and explained the situation. Derick promised he was on his way. A.J. scooped up Bear and brought him into the main house.

"Mr. Clemente!" he shouted.

The startled-looking older man gaited into the kitchen where A.J. gently set Bear on the floor.

Tess's father took one look at Bear and said, "I'll get blankets."

"She's gone," was all A.J. said. "And I can't find Hudson, either."

A look of panic crossed Mr. Clemente's features and then resolve. "You go find her. I'll take good care of your friend here."

He disappeared as A.J. searched his dog's face for any signs of improvement. He leaned toward Bear's ear and whispered, "Don't die on me, buddy. It's you and me, right. We have a lot more time together. I have to go but Derick is on his way. He'll take good care of you along with Mr. Clemente, I promise. Stay with me, buddy."

"Derick's on the way." A.J. had never felt more torn in his life. The only reason he could leave was the fact that Bear had Mr. Clemente to watch over him until Derick arrived but A.J. was Tess's best chance at survival. "I'll call the sheriff."

Mr. Clemente nodded as he wrapped Bear in a blanket.

"I won't let him die. Now, go on," he promised.

Still barefoot, A.J. bolted toward the spot he'd found Bear. On the way, he managed to call the sheriff, who picked up on the first ring.

"Tess is missing. Bear has been poisoned. You're looking for the wrong man. Hudson Leonard is responsible for the murders and he has Tess."

The sheriff muttered a few choice words into the phone. "Where are you?"

"The Clemente ranch. He took her from in front of the barn again." A.J. surveyed the area next to where he'd found Bear. He found the trail again of what looked like a body had been dragged.

"Jesus. I'm on my way."

"I'm heading into the woods. There are marks in the dirt. It looks like he dragged her behind the barn." When A.J. really thought about it, Hudson had the perfect alibi. He was supposed to be inside the house. "Call me when you get here."

"Let me know the minute you find something." He

could hear her panting through the receiver like she was running. He heard a car door open and then shut.

"Okay." He ended the call and pocketed the cell. From the marks in the dirt, a body had been dragged around the side of the barn, blocking the view from the house. There was a pen directly behind the barn.

A.J. followed the footsteps to the woods. He issued a sharp breath. The bastard had taken her into the woods.

Of course he would, When A.J. really thought about it. Hudson would still be trying to sell the lie. He would let this be sold as Rhett circling back to finish the job. It would play perfectly into his obsessive nature.

A.J. rocketed through the trees, ignoring the sticks and rocks stabbing his bare feet. He'd taken a quick shower, so Hudson had to be around here somewhere. It was dark and this property was unfamiliar.

His eyes were adjusting but it would take time. He searched the area, looking for a body hanging from a tree.

Killing her any other way would break the pattern. If Hudson planned to sneak back inside the house, the site must be around there somewhere. Based on the marks behind the barn, Hudson picked her up to carry her. She'd be dead weight and that would be difficult for a man Hudson's size. He probably couldn't carry her for very long.

A.J. slowed his pace and listened, fearing he'd overshot. There was no wind, no breeze rustling through the trees. The woods were alive with the sounds of crickets and katydids.

He circled back, stopping when he heard the sounds of branches snapping. Either a large animal was stalking him, or this was the first sign he was on Hudson's tail.

Having had to track poachers as part of his job on the ranch, A.J. could be stealth in the woods when he needed to be. It would be a helluva lot easier if he knew the land but that was okay.

This bastard had the woman A.J. loved—loved? Yes, he loved her. And all he could think about was bringing Tess home and Bear surviving. The guy was also responsible for Bear's condition. Fire shot through A.J.'s veins at what Hudson was trying to take away.

A.J. stilled and controlled his own breathing. He waited. There was a reason for the saying about patience winning wars. It was true.

And then he heard it. The telltale sound of heavy breathing. Hudson was close. And that meant Tess was, too. A.J. couldn't be certain but he didn't believe enough time had passed for Hudson to do anything with her.

The thought struck that he could've already killed her and stashed the body so he could come back around to it. He'd be risking animals like vultures finding her first. An ME would be able to identify the time of death.

Hudson hadn't planned all this out so meticulously to make a mistake like this. It was brilliant, actually, when A.J. really thought about Hudson's plan. He must've realized his father was sick. He didn't stand to inherit the ranch with Tess still alive. Her father had been clear that she was to inherit the place. She'd been groomed to run Clemente Cattle.

But killing her after their father died would put suspicion directly on Hudson. So, he decides to set up Rhett as a ritualistic killer. No one would believe Rhett was innocent and he didn't have the mental capacity to mount a good defense. He would crack under the pressure, just as he was doing.

Rhett was playing right into Hudson's hands. But then, he figured that would happen all along.

So, he set up ritualistic murders. He carried out the first, which had loose ties to the center. Then, his half-sister was on the agenda. But she got away. So, he killed again and maybe he'd been planning the third murder all along. It was the best way to keep authorities looking for a serial killer who might strike again.

But Hudson was done after the third. He'd killed enough to cover and not get caught. Except the one person he truly needed dead was the one who got away. That must've angered him. His entire plan to gain the Clemente family fortune hinged on Tess dying first.

Rhett Daniels was expendable to Hudson. The perfect patsy.

Hudson must believe that months later, long after Rhett was locked up, Mr. Clemente would die from the cancer slowly killing him. He'd been hiding his illness and was the type of person who would keep it under wraps until the very end.

Hudson would stand to inherit the ranch. If A.J. had to guess, Hudson's logistic business wasn't as successful as Tess believed.

The heavy breather came closer. A.J. slowly and stealthily positioned himself behind a tree. He squatted down, ready to spring at Hudson as he passed by.

The breather stopped. He muttered a curse.

A.J. realized the guy was lost.

There was no use waiting. Hudson was close enough for A.J. to strike. He came around the tree trunk in a flash, diving straight into Hudson's knees. Hudson took a step backward. Holding Tess knocked him off balance.

In another second, A.J. grabbed Tess from over Hudson's shoulder. He eased her down onto the ground, taking a couple of fists to his back and head. And then Hudson got the bright idea to run.

"It won't do any good, Hudson. The sheriff is on her way." A.J. moved with ease through the thicket. This time when he tackled Hudson, the man went down like a forty-foot tree in logging country.

Hudson twisted around, grunting as he tried to gouge A.J. in the eyes.

"I hope it was worth it, Hudson. You're going to be locked up for the rest of your life," A.J. said.

"This is for Bear, by the way." A.J. reared his fist back and then slammed it into Hudson's face. He felt something wet on his knuckles and figured he'd just broken the guy's nose.

It also made him worry about Rhett.

More of that fire raged through A.J. but he needed to contain himself as he squeezed Hudson's torso in between powerful thighs. One by one, A.J. forced the guys arms at his sides, pinning him with his legs.

"I'm suing you, asshole. He's probably getting away with my sister right now."

"Right. Your sister. The person you care so much about. You can drop the act with me, Hudson. I know exactly what you've done and what you're capable of. I also know the only way you can overpower someone is to surprise them by knocking them out from behind. That's a coward move, Hudson."

"She deserves everything she was about to get," he spit out angrily.

"I hope the money was worth spending the rest of your life behind bars," A.J. shot back.

"You think this is just about money?" Hudson laughed and it sounded like pure evil. "That bitch was always our dad's favorite. She doesn't even like the family business, but that wasn't stopping her from learning it. I'm just taking what should be mine and punishing that old bastard for ignoring me and Mom."

"So this is revenge against Tess?"

"No, it's revenge against him. Watching his precious daughter die at the hands of a true sicko was his worst fear. It's the main reason he didn't want her working in social work. I wanted *him* to suffer before he died. I wanted him to live out the rest of his days knowing his precious Tess had been tortured and then killed by a psycho. That's the ultimate revenge. Taking his money is just icing on the cake." Hudson's face had been transformed by hate. His eyebrows were slashes now and the lines of his forehead were scored deep.

A.J. squeezed his thighs harder and it literally took every ounce of self-discipline he had not to put the guy's lights out permanently. Hudson Leonard deserved to live out the rest of his considerably long life doing hard time.

"It was once said that a man who desires revenge should dig two graves. But since death is too easy an out for you, I'm going to enjoy watching you try to survive in prison. Those inmates are going to love someone like you." A.J. managed to pull out his cell and make the call to the sheriff, giving her the best directions he could.

He heard a groaning noise in the direction he'd left Tess.

"Tess, sweetheart, I'm here. You're going to be okay."

Hudson started to say something that A.J. assumed

would be a nasty remark, so he punched the guy with enough force to knock him out.

"Bear," a raspy voice said, Tess's voice.

"He's with your dad," was all A.J. had the heart to say.

"A.J."

"I'm here, sweetheart."

"My...it was..."

"Save your energy. Hudson isn't going anywhere, and help is on the way." It took everything inside A.J. not to run to her. But he wouldn't risk this bastard waking up and crawling away.

It didn't take long for noises and lights to descend on the area.

"Over here," A.J. shouted.

Sheriff Justice came running. Out of breath, but with handcuffs on the ready.

"I knocked him out cold, but he'll wake up soon enough." A.J. pushed up, jabbing his knee into Hudson's stomach one last time as he got to his feet.

"I have him now, A.J. Great work." The sheriff immediately rolled him onto his stomach and jerked his hands behind his back. He was cuffed in a matter of seconds. She pulled a packet out of her pocket, broke it in half, and then place it under his nose.

His face wrinkled but Hudson's eyes opened.

A.J. couldn't get to Tess fast enough. An EMT was there, helping her sit up against a tree.

"I'm right here, Tess." And if she'd have him, he would never leave.

"A.J." A smile ghosted her lips.

He searched her body for any signs of blood.

"Can you tell me what day it is?" the EMT asked.

"Sunday," she replied, and she was one for one.

"What's your name, darlin'?" he continued.

"Tess Nicole Clemente."

Two for two.

"I'm Jake and I'm going to be taking care of you, okay?" Jake palmed a small flashlight. "Look at me."

She did and he shined the light in her eye.

"Okay, look at your boyfriend over there," Jake said.

Tess shifted her gaze to A.J.

"Good." He checked her pulse and then asked, "Does it hurt anywhere?"

"My head." She pointed to the left of the crown of her head.

"Mind if I take a look?" Jake asked.

"Go ahead. I'd say knock yourself out but..." She cracked a smile and A.J. finally let out the breath he'd been holding.

She gasped and turned toward A.J. "Bear. Is he okay?"

"Vet is working on him now." He didn't want to make the call in front of her, in case the news wasn't great. Wanting to get back to his best buddy was a physical ache. In a best-case scenario, Tess would be cleared and the two of them could be by Bear's side.

The EMT finished his examination by tucking his instruments inside his bag. He put his hands on his thighs and said, "I advise going to the hospital to be checked out more thoroughly.

She shook her head and winced. "I need to know if Bear is okay. I'm fine. Or I will be. I want to be there for him the way he's been there for me."

The EMT nodded. "Any chance I can talk you out of this?"

"Nope. I promise to swing by the doc's office tomorrow. Other than a headache, I'll be fine," she said.

"If that changes, go straight to the hospital." He didn't look at Tess, his gaze locked onto to A.J. "If she stops making sense, do you promise to run her in?"

"Absolutely," A.J. promised. Taking care of Tess and Bear were his top priorities at the moment.

"Then, I'm done here. Do you need help getting back to the house?" Jake looked at A.J.'s feet. "I can check those out for you while we're here."

A.J. looked down and saw all the scrapes.

"Nah, I'll take care of them in the house." All he needed was a little soap and antibiotic ointment and he'd be right as rain.

Jake popped to his feet. "At least let me lend you a pair of slippers."

"Those, I'll take."

With Jake's help, A.J. managed to get Tess safely out of the woods. The sheriff walked Hudson out. The look on his face was priceless when he realized how long he was going to be locked away for his crimes.

Mr. Clemente met them at the back door. The stoic look on his face had been replaced with concern. He glanced from A.J. to Tess and back. "Thank you."

A.J. nodded.

"Derick moved him into Tess's room. He's working on him now." Mr. Clemente stepped aside to allow passage.

A.J. kept his arm around Tess for the walk and she leaned more of her weight on him.

He knocked on the door before entering. Seeing Bear lying on his side with an IV coming out of him scored a direct hit in the center of his chest. It felt like a bomb had detonated.

"There was no time to take him off property. Since I knew what I was walking into, I grabbed supplies on my way out," he started. "But the news you're waiting to hear is that he'll pull through this." Derick stood up and turned around. "You got to him in time."

"That's some of the best news I've heard all day," A.J. said.

Tess beamed up at him as she hugged him a little tighter and for a split-second, the crazy mixed-up world that had tilted on its axis righted itself again.

"The fluids will wash out the rest of the poison. At his size, it probably would've taken a larger dose to kill him, but it came close." Derick gathered up his supplies. "If you'll excuse me. I'll come back to check on him in a few hours. Once that bag finishes drip-ping, you can take it out yourself or call and I'll come do it."

"I got this, Derick. Thanks. Go on home. You can come back in the morning. If anything changes with him, I'll call." A.J. had pulled out his fair share of IVs over the years. He knew exactly what to do.

With Tess by his side, A.J. moved to the bed. Bear's tail immediately started wagging. Tess took the chair that had been pulled up next to the bed and A.J. sat down with his dog.

"Good boy, Bear." He leaned over and rested his head next to Bear's. "You have a lot of living left to do."

That night, A.J. and Tess slept curled up next to Bear.

Tess was the first one to wake the next morning. She slipped into the bathroom to freshen up.

The door opened and A.J. walked in. "Okay if I join you in here?"

She nodded as she finished brushing her teeth.

"Where's Bear?"

"Outside with your father. They seem to be bond-ing." A.J. moved next to her and grabbed a toothbrush and toothpaste.

Tess watched as he stood there, looking so right in her bathroom at the sink next to her.

He rinsed out his mouth and turned to her with a look of concern.

"What's wrong?"

Oh, man. How did she tackle that question? How did she tell him that the only time nothing was wrong was when she was with him and Bear?

She figured it was now or never and she might as well develop the courage to say what had been on her mind.

"A.J. McGannon, if someone told me last week that I'd be standing here in this spot with you, I would've laughed in their face. But now? I find myself in the unexpected position of not wanting to leave." She studied him and he gave no indication of what he was feeling. His face was a stone, and a gorgeous one at that. She wanted to be able to look into those gorgeous hazel-brown eyes for the rest of her life and if she stopped now she feared she would never have the bravery to tell him what he really meant to her.

She'd stepped aside and let her father run her life for too long. And that was on her. Caring about someone else's feelings was one thing. Now, she realized anyone who loved her would want the best for her. It might take some getting used to, but her father would come around. He wouldn't spend the time he had left unhappy with her.

So, she continued.

"I've fallen for you hard, A.J. I'm in love with you."

He stood there looking a little stunned.

When he didn't respond, her pulse shot through the roof and her heart pounded the inside of her rib cage, beating out a staccato rhythm.

There it was. She'd put her feelings out there. The thought of him rejecting her pressed a heavy weight on her shoulders that she doubted she'd recover from.

Maybe she should've played it cool. He'd made it pretty obvious that his feelings for her went beyond friendship. She could have waited to see how it all played out.

But then hadn't she been doing that her whole life? Standing in the background, taking what life gave instead of grabbing the bull by the horns.

"What do you think about the two of us making a go of it?" she asked, unable to make eye contact.

Her confidence was short-lived when he didn't immediately respond. Her heart freefell, slamming into her toes. If he didn't feel the same, it was time to buck up.

She forced her chin up. It was important to know where she stood with him. Anything less than a real shot at a relationship wouldn't be good enough anyway.

A moment of hesitation struck. She wished he would say something instead of looking like he was trying to find the right words.

Tess knew exactly what she wanted even if he didn't. And since she'd already showed her cards, she figured that she might as well go all-in. If it didn't go her way, she would learn to accept it. She could always request to work with a different family member when a dispute came up to ease the awkwardness they would both feel now. The McGannons were decent people and would understand the basis of her request.

"Say something," she urged, looking away. Somehow, facing a different direction seemed like it would help soften the blow when he told her that he didn't love her and didn't want to speak to her again.

Instead, he took a knee.

Tess's mouth fell open and shock robbed her voice.

"Tess Clemente, I'd intended to speak with your father first but here we are, and this seems like the best possible moment to tell you how I feel."

Her arms goose bumped, and warmth spread through her.

"I couldn't love anyone more than I love you. You're the sun when the world is full of clouds. You've become my best friend and the person I most want to talk to when anything happens in my life. There's always been something undeniable between us and now I finally figured out what it is...love." He took her hand in his. "Would you do me the great honor of becoming my equal partner in life? Tess Clemente, will you marry me?"

He hadn't finished his sentence before Tess had cupped his face in her hands. With tears of joy in her eyes, she said, "Yes, A.J., I'll marry you."

A.J. was on his feet in a split-second. He looped his arms around her. And she kissed him.

Mouths fused in the sweetest kiss she'd ever experienced.

He pulled back first and, breathless, said, "I always knew you were a game-changer. I just didn't know what that meant until now."

"You're my home, A.J."

And she meant it. With A.J., she'd found home.

17

The camera was set. The equipment in place. The wedding would stream into Clive McGannon's hospital room where Kurt sat along with his new brother Levi.

"We were gathered at the hospital the other day because he moved his fingers," Levi said, looking at his father—a man Kurt felt no magic connection to despite learning they were related.

What had he expected?

A sudden blast in his heart that said, *Hey, that guy's my father*?

Kurt wouldn't even be here if it wasn't for a kinky-haired angel back at home. His one-year-old daughter, Paisley, owned his heart. She deserved to have more of a family than just Kurt. Losing her mother and the woman Kurt had spent more than half of his life loving had brought him to his knees.

He reminded himself that he was here for Paisley. His feelings—or lack of them toward the McGannons—didn't matter. His daughter had more uncles than she'd know what to do with. Of course, he had no plans to rush introductions. He needed to make darn sure they would treat her the way she deserved and not like an outsider.

"We are gathered here together today..." the minister's voice boomed from the laptop speakers. The device had been positioned on a table so that Mr. McGannon could watch the ceremony in case he opened his eyes.

There was so much hope in the faces of his sons and nephews. A man with this much family surrounding him must've done something right in his life. It didn't give him a free pass for the fact he'd turned his back on Kurt and his mother, but it did interest him.

Kurt was lost in thought as the ceremony continued in the background. The constant beeps of machinery keeping Clive McGannon alive became white noise after sitting there for a while.

He checked back into the wedding at the pronunciation of man and wife before the kiss. Spacing out kept him from thinking back to his wedding day to Stacy. She'd worn a beautiful white dress that he'd later learned was a rental.

They barely had two nickels to rub together in the beginning of their marriage, but they'd been happy.

They'd been good together. There wasn't a day that went by that he didn't think about her. Wish she could hold their daughter or that he could go to her for advice on a million things relating to Paisley.

"My brother Ryan and I are waiting for Dad to wake up before our official weddings. A.J. and Tess moved forward so her father could be present. He's ill and doesn't have a whole lot of time left," Levi broke into Kurt's thoughts.

"What's A.J. doing?" Kurt watched as he handed over a piece of paper.

Tess opened it, read it, and then wrapped her arms around her husband's neck.

"Her father asked us to buy his ranch to secure her future. That's A.J. giving her back the deed. We voted and decided the land should stay with Tess and her father," Levi informed.

This news shattered Kurt's initial judgment of the McGannons. He figured most people as rich as them were just as ruthless.

"She doesn't want to tend to the herd, so we're taking over that part. We felt the land that she and her father loved would always belong to her and A.J.'s children." Levi pinched the bridge of his nose. "Now, if Dad would just wake up. The family would be complete."

"You and your father are close?" Kurt asked.

"Yeah. We're all pretty tightknit, though. I doubt Dad has a favorite," Levi admitted.

Kurt didn't know the man, so those words shouldn't hurt as much as they did.

"Aren't you upset with him? I mean, you had to have done the math by now. I know I did. Our mothers were pregnant at the same time. Since he was married to yours, it seems obvious he had an affair," Kurt said. "That doesn't make you mad?"

Levi nodded. "It did at first. But, you know, relationships are complicated and if Dad could speak, he might be able to clear this up. I'm trying to hold judgment until I hear his side of the story."

Math was still math, and the numbers told their own story. Kurt held his tongue, though. If Levi McGannon wanted to live in denial, Kurt didn't want to be the one to burst the man's bubble.

"I heard about her half-brother," Kurt nodded toward the screen. Technically, he'd read about the crimes in the news.

"Hudson tried to plea bargain but was denied. The man is going to Huntsville with all the other hardened criminals where he will stay the rest of his life," Levi said. "Her dad said that he should've known something was up when Hudson seemed desperate for money a couple of times. Tess said her half-brother seemed interested in her work, so she didn't question when he asked about her clients. She never mentioned names, but it was probably easy for him to put two-and-two together after visiting the center. The man is sick."

"That's messed up," Kurt agreed.

"I mean, money is just that. Paper. Zeroes in a bank. I'm not diminishing the need to put food on the table. Beyond that, it doesn't bring real happiness or love," Levi stated.

"Growing up without any was tough, but we made do. We were happy enough." Kurt couldn't agree more now that he had a little money of his own. Beyond being able to pay his mortgage and put food on the table, having more cash in the bank didn't create a magic well of happiness.

"Well, today is about a celebration," Levi said, and it was obvious he was trying to redirect the conversation. "What about you? Anyone special in your life?"

"Nah. My daughter and my business are all I have time for," he said, shaking his head.

Kurt couldn't imagine finding someone that he could love as much as he'd loved his wife. He'd grabbed the brass ring, held onto it and had everything he could've ever wanted in a person.

Then, she died.

And now he had a booming business and an amazing kid. He was so tired some nights that he didn't make it to his bed. Crashing on the couch had become habit.

In his life, there wasn't room for anything else.

To READ Kurt and Arianna's story, click here.

ALSO BY BARB HAN

Kidnapped at Christmas

Murder and Mistletoe

Bulletproof Christmas

For more of Barb's books, visit www.BarbHan.com.

ABOUT THE AUTHOR

Barb Han is a USA TODAY and Publisher's Weekly Bestselling Author. Reviewers have called her books "heartfelt" and "exciting."

Barb lives in Texas—her true north—with her adventurous family, a poodle mix and a spunky rescue who is often referred to as a hot mess. She is the proud owner of too many books (if there is such a thing). When not writing, she can be found exploring Manhattan, on a mountain either hiking or skiing depending on the season, or swimming in her own backyard.

Sign up for Barb's newsletter at www.BarbHan.com.